D1740806

RIPCORD

Nate Lippens is the author of the novel *My Dead Book* (Publication Studio, 2021 and Pilot Press, 2022), a finalist for The Republic of Consciousness Prize. His fiction has appeared in the anthologies *Little Birds* (Filthy Loot, 2021), *Responses to Derek Jarman's Blue* (Pilot Press, 2022) and *Pathetic Literature*, edited by Eileen Myles (Grove, 2022).

RIPCORD

Nate Lippens

PILOT PRESS

For Emily

1

Some people get the glory. Some people get the glory hole.

I remember when I was young spying an old man—probably forty—sitting at a gay bar in short shorts and a tank top, smoking with the slow-mo of a 1970s movie, like he had all the time in the world. When the door opened, he appraised new arrivals. I examined his get-up, his fussy little gestures, and his longing stare with repulsion. To be so old and still on the prowl.

Now I'm well past his age and I can bring the prowl to my door. And I do.

I am the age where young men's daddy issues work to my advantage, but I can't bankroll my end of the deal. I am stuck with the truly damaged seeking validation or abuse or abusive validation. *Bring the belt* one messaged. The next morning my hand was swollen. I'd sprained it spanking a low-level brand strategist in a designer jockstrap. I told my friend Charlie about the injury. I'd once loaned him money for the dentist after he chipped his tooth on a wedding band at a glory hole. Charlie said, "Why not age disgracefully? I mean, have you seen what passes for dignity? For us, it's always been an awkward age."

***

After a disaster date with a guy who said, "I guess I thought you were butch by your photo," I changed my profile to: 5'7" fem with the face of an embittered sea captain, the voice of a pissed-off fey concierge, and a body like an unmade bed.

***

I've never maintained a romantic relationship for more than two years. I don't have children or pets, and I recently purchased, nurtured, and murdered a cactus.

An acquaintance asks if I'm dating anyone. He has a friend in mind. I say I'm retired. I came out at fourteen which means I have more than thirty years of being out. I should be able to retire. I don't expect a watch, maybe an acknowledgment: *Thanks for your service.* Maybe a moment of silence. I am simply done. I'm not good at romantic life. I make bad decisions and stick with them. Loyalty to poor judgment is one of my most pronounced character traits. I am bowing out too late to have any honor but before I cause more harm. Not exactly noble but at least belatedly honest.

***

I have so vigorously rejected my role as gay side-kick/
agony aunt that when someone tried to tell me about
their marital problems this week, I said, "Are you
hitting on me?"

***

"Imagine a life without shame," Charlie says.

"I believe that's called death."

Charlie is not a hugger. We have both joked about
being raised by wire-monkey mothers. I once explained
my mostly forgotten childhood to him this way: "When I
was about six, my paternal grandmother told a group of
church women I had introduced hugging to our family."

***

My friend's thirteen-year-old daughter asks why I never
married. I tell her I haven't found the right one. I don't
say marriage didn't exist as an option when I was
young, and I learned to think and live outside all those
situations. I don't say part of rejecting the victim's
badge was turning what I was taught was wrong and

disgusting about me into excess and glory. Make trauma into refusal. Things have changed, as my fuck buddy Dustin says, but I can't undo a lifetime. Later I teach my friend's daughter how to play triple-peak solitaire. "I'm good at this," I say. "And the best part is no one knows."

***

Soft targets: Me lying in bed awake wishing I knew how to tell the man sleeping next to me what it was like to be in my head but knowing that would mean he wouldn't love me anymore. That knowledge meant I couldn't love him either. In the end, I had to tell him. I didn't want to hurt him, but I knew I would. He cried but I didn't hold him. I meant for the pain to be quick. I'd rehearsed for days beforehand. Once it was happening my words were an echo. He asked how long I hadn't been in love with him. I talked around the answer because there was a fine line between honesty and cruelty.

***

People say they want *honesty* and *authenticity*, but *not this*. I admit my faults. If they insist on them from a place of superiority, what they imagine as moral or ethical, I enumerate their reciprocal faults according to their own standards. Yes, I am fragile and erratic, and you are a serial monogamist reenacting your childhood abuse and abandonment in a looping series of relationships that are codependent, cruel, and, worst of all, boring.

***

The number of texts I have typed and deleted this morning: five. Expression outpaces doubt but doubt has the final word (silence). I await disaster. I mean Dustin's text. His messages are too short or run-on with drink and maudlin words. A voice talking to itself. Fantasies talking to other fantasies. What concerns me is wanting them. Clearly, they need no one. A loop intelligible for the length of a tinny anthem, then dark.

***

I station myself where the bar curves, riveted by performances of unembarrassed need. All around me it's duck-duck-goose, misery-misery-magnificence, obsession-obsession-disappointment. A man moves through the bar

like he's panhandling for cock. An older man—my age—
has a younger man buttonholed by the corner mirror.
Sugar Pop's eyes are like a 150-watt bulb screwed into a
small reading lamp: it hurts to look at them.

Beside me two men are sparring or flirting.

"You're hurting my feelings."

"You have feelings?'

"I do. I have a sensitive side."

"The shaft of your cock doesn't count."

In the mirror behind the bar, I'm not bad. Might
be good to have a body beside me, something solid to
keep me from floating away. Not a smart idea. But this
isn't a thought. It's blood moving around.

***

Dustin finishes and hunts around for his smokes. I stand
with my jeans still unbuttoned, grab the pack of cigarettes and lighter, which have slipped behind the
couch cushion, and hand them over.

Dustin fumbles one from the pack and concen-
trates on the flame.

I button up and walk to the bathroom where my
wild face slides into the mirror's view. Back to the

living room, Dustin, coat on, wavers as he leashes his dog, a scrubby mop named Angie.

"Dickinson?" I asked upon introduction.

He looked confused. "You mean Emily?"

Never mind.

He told me Angie was named after a friend who died. What a hell of a tribute. Picking up shit in memory.

"I'll walk you down. Angie needs to go out."

The words are slurry yet determined. Dustin wants me to clear out. His husband will be home from work soon.

***

I wear Leo's blue and black checked flannel shirt—an XL that drowns me—and remember leaning against him and resting my head against his shoulder.

Three springs ago, snow still patchy on the ground, I smoked by a woodpile and hitched up Leo's long johns, which I was wearing. I thought of his body and the cigarette keeping me from it. A big man with a beard and long hair. For an atheist, I sure have dated a lot of men who look like Jesus. Leo was hot. On an actual body temperature level. Wrapped around me, I sweated under his heat, like I might dissolve.

Cigarette finished, back in bed, Leo kissed my forehead. He held my face in his hands and said, "I'm going to give you a beautiful life." I wanted what he said, wanted to believe, but then a blip-thought: Why must you lie to us both? And also: Who do you think you are?

Leo was a foot taller than me. One night, we fetched the soft tape measure and laid it all out—thigh circumference, knee to groin, forearm length, clavicle to navel, ball hang in a seventy-degree room in January—and wrote the numbers in a grid notebook.

Months later we were in the dark. The end of a long night.

"We're going in different directions," he said.

The fact he thought I had a direction broke my heart.

"We'll figure it out," I said.

"I already have. This isn't working out."

The heat drained from me. Not a wisp of love in his voice. Efficient, businesslike. I wanted to be far away from its rounded baritone gone flat as Nebraska. Many mornings I'd been in the same spot listening to water run in the bathroom. Sometimes I'd gone in and joined. Once when Leo had gone to work and left me in his apartment sleeping, I woke, picked up the paperback on the nightstand, and opened it to see his neat signature on the flyleaf. Such schoolboy claims made me smile. I wanted to be his book.

A string of worn and worthless words ran together. Phrases dumb people made to break up with other dumb people.

I stood and it was as if I'd never been there at all. In the dark I couldn't see the ripple on Leo's bed where I'd been. I dressed. Moving to leave, I heard my name twice as I closed the door. The hallway was bright and blurry. I took the stairs so I wouldn't risk being in the elevator riding down with other people leaving other beds.

I know how to leave, and I know how to stay, but I have not understood anyone else's reasons for leaving or staying.

Leo once told me it was better to be rejected for who you are than to be loved for who you are not. Both demonstrated a sense of solid self I couldn't relate to. I had spent too much time trying to find a place in the world—sometimes literally a roof over my head—that the luxury of imagining rejection as a choice was laughable. I had mistaken many people for friends, for kindred spirits, not understanding they had chosen to leave conventional life, and I'd been thrown out. They could go back, and they carried the values like shrapnel. I had different wounds that reacted to different weather and there was no going back.

**

Thirty years ago, when the first man I was in love with broke up with me, I left Seattle and took the train to Chicago. I'd never seen much of the west and was in no hurry to arrive and face my confusion. A teenager and her baby sat beside me. She was headed home to Iowa after breaking up with the baby's father. Her parents didn't know she was coming or that they had a grandson. Twice she left the infant with me to go smoke when the train stopped. Third time she left I told him a story, some bastardization of Peter Rabbit, and realized the train was moving again and she hadn't returned. An hour passed and I entertained the idea she had abandoned her son, and I would keep him. The girl returned. "I met a guy, and we hung out in the club car." The next day in Iowa, I said farewell to my almost son and wished his mother luck. We didn't exchange information because I wanted to pretend things would turn out for us.

***

The night: dark and breathing. Him: a dancer's bearing, light and deliberate. Sidewalk gait. Colored lights stipple his face.

***

Are we mostly paper dolls to one another? A row of silhouettes with food allergies, kinks, and gripes?

***

Last summer, the man I hooked up with liked to be choked and slapped. He told me happiness was a choice and there were two types of people—those who talked about money and those who liked toilet humor. He found both distasteful. I enjoyed hitting him.

***

I understand how someone who was once considered beautiful struggles as they age. I understand not because I am compassionate or kind, but because I see they are experiencing loss and I have always lived in the place they are now relegated to. I can't extend a welcome, though, because there is no meeting ground. They remember where they came from, and I remember where they came from too. I'm only visible to them now. I saw them all along.

***

Avery shows me the profile for the guy who gave him herpes. Under the herpes guy's name: I have a HUNGER for freedom. A PASSION for helping and DESIRE to spread good. "Good." We both laugh.

***

I watch Hugh age: crepey elbow, sunspots, thinning hair. This year his neck changed. My hand smooths his rogue eyebrow hairs. We've slept together on and off for decades. He holds me because he can and he's always known how, since we were fifteen-year-olds in the attic of a house under foreclosure. Now we are two middle-aged men in a hotel room. Morning turns black to gray rain, and Hugh sleeps with his arm across me. I remember what it is to love someone even if love is in the past. I mean romantic love. The rest of love pours from everything, emanating from bad furniture and cheap heavy draperies and car horns five floors below. They all conduct the feeling so it can be lost. Hugh stirs, rolls on his side, and it all breaks apart, as it should.

2

I'm in an abusive relationship with time. I haven't left my apartment in a week. I'm embarrassed to say it but not to live it. I wouldn't call my self-exile a withdrawal. I've been through withdrawal a few times and that was about missing something, wanting something I couldn't have anymore. I do not feel that way about people.

***

When I was young, I moved so frequently every address was a forwarding address. My broken heart then was my family. Now it's everything else: the faint echo of all the other ones. Greer calls this the Chamber. A room one enters where the present and the past are if not indistinguishable, then blurred beyond recognition.

You're peripatetic someone once said. I knew of people who called themselves travelers and were always looking for adventure. What I mean is they had money. Not on them. Back home. Money from home. I didn't have money and the people back home didn't have money and they didn't want to hear from me anyway.

***

Home has been such a strange word for me. For years, I have referred to where I grew up as a child as my mother's home. The distinction flies past most people but sticks out to the right ones.

Fifteen. The summer before I left, my mother drove in silence, and I talked. We were going in circles. That building was definitely on repeat. We were lost but she wouldn't admit it. I stopped talking so she could focus, as if she had been paying attention to me, as if that was the problem. Finally, she said, "This isn't working." I thought she meant the drive. Then it hung in the dusted air: Us. Me and her. My mother was working up to dumping me.

After I left, my mother told people I'd ran away. She didn't want to be the woman who kicked her kid out, so she got to be abandoned. I didn't want to be a victim, the kid thrown out of his mom's house. What good would that do? At best, a bed somewhere for a while and pity. At worst, the vampires who smelled desperation and descended. My mother and I both got what we wanted.

***

As someone who spent years having to code switch and lie to survive, when I hear people brag about their authenticity and honesty, I hear *privileged and lazy*.

***

All the years of ricocheting around have left a permanent mark. I will always be restless. When I was younger, I thought it was bad, a character flaw. But I've witnessed how people cave in, lard up, and dull down. I'm not ready for that slow death march. I still want things, ridiculously small yet unlikely dreams I've kept flickering for twenty years. Maybe something can turn out. Something so tiny it won't change anything. Why not? People have crazier and more mundane plans they turn into crusades trumpeting through lives.

***

Another move, another unpack. I rifle through a box and find an envelope of photos and slides of me at sixteen with a bleached blond grown-out mohawk. I suppose this is the moment where someone my age says, "Who was that person?" or smiles with amusement at their youth, but I hold all that rage and fear still, fresh as ever. A fact more real than this box. I have seen people post pictures of themselves laughingly from their pasts. *I thought I was so punk*, says the caption, written from an office or home, somewhere safer, distant. I scroll through their vacation and food photos and think, how boring. How did I waste my time on people killing theirs until their marriages, mortgages, and affairs arrived?

***

Avery tells me I'm not working-class. To him, working-class means a CNC machinist.

I look at my reflection in the screen and say, "Elite."

***

How do I talk to a person who has never been so hungry they've considered mugging someone?

***

A friend was kept by a rich boyfriend and given a monthly allowance he referred to as "walking around money." I believe it was four grand. That's a hell of walk. The keeper and the allowance came to an end. There was a severance payment. The friend drifted around New York for a year or two, making and breaking plans, reeling in and throwing back suitors of means. Eventually he left for a trip to California and didn't return. Rumors of Los Angeles and hard, harder, and hardest drugs followed, as well as tidbits about ashrams and a desert community of artists. Then a few years ago walking uptown I thought I saw him, a version of him with a tautened face, eating in a bistro. The face looked at me, the space of maybe a glance, and looked away quickly. Recognition or not, him or not, I quickened my pace.

***

My unconscious is not subtle: dreams of lottery winnings, expensive boots, and rough sex. Where are those cryptic encoded ones other people share? Or are they lying?

***

Bills don't stop even when it feels like time has. You get up and go to work. A terrible job but a job for now, desperately needed money to get out of the place you live and move somewhere less desperate, less temporary. You don't even think about living in a good place or calling it home because that's childish. Privacy is only the space you make in your head and even that is small. The things happening are bad enough you know you will feel new afterward.

***

My happy hour shift at the Dilly Dally is full of them. People who believe they gave everything and got nothing and people who gave nothing and got everything. They hate each other but they sit beside one another, bonded in misery, and if they could swap places, they would still be here drinking.

Late afternoon bar: Sports on the TV and oldies Midwestern arena rock with a twang playing. Verses of hardship, confusion, lost love, dreams deferred, lift into choruses of defiance and triumph. How often has defiance, real defiance, ended in triumph? I don't mean stubbornness in the face of shitty choices, I mean standing alone with no support—family, school, religion—

and challenging their blind authority to erase you? In movies, songs, history books—sure. In life, I haven't experienced or witnessed even one.

***

Whoever said there is no such thing as bad publicity had family money.

***

Catered for young rich people today. Home now, changed into my nightshirt, lantern turned low, telling the shadows about how Marie Antoinette stepped on her executioner's foot walking to the guillotine. Her last words: "Pardonnez-moi, monsieur." The shadows love that story.

***

My only life advice: Silver-service food is served from the left. Drinks and plated meals are served from the right. The guest to the host's right is served first.

***

They swim smugly with the current in a river dug for them and tell us how easy it is. They wear $500 Heritage work boots in black-cherry leather and $300 plaid shirts. Class anxiety is expensive.

***

Kill the rich (no exceptions—sorry) reads the graffiti. I agree but I don't think I should kill anyone. Not because of any moral reason. It's too late to say murder is wrong. (I've been walking on graves my whole life. So have you.) If I started killing, I wouldn't know where to stop. Kill a man and you have to kill his family so no one tries to avenge him. Then you have to kill his friends, kill his family's friends, and the friends' friends and all their families. Pets too. Obviously, kill all priests and politicians. All leaders. Their followers. The terrible Christians from my childhood. If Jesus returns, finish him too. Too late to the party, Christ. I would be a killing machine and I don't want to be a machine. Not more than I am now. A killer? The killer? Fine, fine. But a killing machine? No thanks. Covered in blood and gunshot residue. All DNA and ballistic evidence. A walking crime scene. Sure, it's sexy but it's so much work and there are new assholes born every minute.

My work would never be done. *No exceptions — sorry.* A life of death dealing. A life of parenthetical grudge.

***

Dear Citibank, I assure you the credit score you are offering may be free, but it will not be complimentary.

There aren't enough hours in the day to say no to all the all the things I don't want to do.

I want to run away and leave everything. I check my bank account and settle for cold pizza and a book.

***

I worked brunch and am icing my knees and praying to Satan for sleep or sudden death. The shift was both boring and fraught. A coworker referred to me as a seasoned pro in a way that suggested a past rife with drifters who tipped in venison and scratch-off lottery tickets. I overheard a man say, "If there is a No Firearms sign, I get back in my truck and go somewhere else. The missus and I don't eat in free fire zones." The cokehead line cook said dairy congested him. He explained how wheat turned to sugar in the body and how sugar broke down collagen and accelerated aging. He looked right at me. I excused myself to smoke.

***

Greer tells me the name of the envoy Queen Victoria dispatched to meet Karl Marx: Sir Mountstuart Elphinstone Grant Duff.

***

The oldest story: An insider pretends to be an outsider and receives praise for his empathy and imagination and intelligence. Maybe some asshole even says bravery. An outsider pretends to be an insider, is exposed as a fraud, a liar, and burned to the ground.

***

Time and again I outwitted my destiny. I freed myself from my family of farmers and factory workers. My faggotry was my passport. It allowed me to rise above my social class. I dodged the boredom of its implicit victimhood through rage and drugs. I moved constantly. I evaded community and friends who wanted to replicate family roles. I left jobs and towns. I didn't stay in touch. I made myself, unmade myself, started over from scratch. I am my own creator, so yes, I do believe in god.

I am an institutionally illegitimate person and I conduct myself accordingly. When I think of who are considered credible witnesses and reliable sources and *good* people, I don't want to be aligned with them. I am not good. I'm not on the side of that at all. I'll stay over here with the ex-cons and former junkies and dropouts and fuckups.

***

That's the deck. This is the hand. What can you do?

3

I've peaked as an elder queer, chewing Nicorette, pulling my metal grocery cart up to my building where a young tenant cries on the stoop, and asking him, "What's wrong, honey?"

I'm in my laundry day attire of army surplus pants, Alan Vega tee, old boots ready for donation to the Smithsonian as Civil War relics. *Dream baby dream*.

The tenant sniffles about a man. "I'll be okay."

"Of course, you will."

"Do you see anything about new love in my life?"

"Oh no, you misunderstood. I'm not psychic. I once had a psychotic break during a major depression."

A block away, I run into a young junkie queen I've only encountered at night. Once as I returned home with takeout, he pointed at it and grimaced, "Food?"

I said, "French fries. I'm not sure that's food."

"Oh, I love French fries, chocolate pudding, and pink champagne."

Today he says, "What are you doing outside in the sun?" and helpfully points to the sky.

"Letting the world see what it's missing."

***

Charlie lost his job last year and rented out the spare room in his house. His roommate is a constant source of complaint.

"The cat destroyed a roll of toilet paper, but he insists on still using it," Charlie says. "Every crap is like a Mummenschanz routine."

Charlie says his roommate doesn't know who Mummenschanz is.

"He's thirty. What are you going to test him on next? The Katzenjammer Kids? The Kipper Kids? Bugs Bunny in drag in the Looney Tunes' *Hillbilly Hare*?"

This is the problem: We are old and broke, and we are relegated to the limbo of intergenerational interactions to survive. Miscommunications and agitations abound. A sense of being not so much past our prime— we are—as cast out of time, running alongside it. A bus that clearly saw us but sped by our stop.

***

Charlie fetched all of his boxes out of storage to sort, sell, and toss. They are time capsules. A CD of Exene Cervenka reading excerpts from the Unabomber Manifesto.

"1996? I think I got this at Fireside Bowl when Auntie Christ played."

Charlie and I met in Chicago back when he wrote for *Punk Planet* and *P-form*, the performance art journal, staged weird shit at Lower Links, attended homocore shows at the Fireside Bowl, and put out poetry chapbooks.

Our world then was punk-house shows and dive bars where beloved bands parked borrowed station wagons with a U-Haul trailer in tow and caused a racket. White guys stood in the front and pointed their forefingers at the singer and yelled back the lyrics. A holler-off. The yelping singer spittled the microphone. The pit collided like atoms in a centrifuge. Depending on my mood and drug intake it was either an inbred circuit or a movie yet to be storyboarded.

Charlie remembers when he used to send off a cashier's check to a post office box in England to get a record he'd only read about. The closeted drummer we both fucked who day-jobbed as a butcher. Nom de punk: the Cleaver.

Dusk added the earth to the sky. In Charlie's car with a mixtape of favorite rage-alongs playing, we cruised around. He pointed to a passing house. "Russ Terrible lives there." Only later did I realize he'd said

Russ Terrill. The mishearing stuck and when the story was retold to Russ, he adopted the name. Alter egos, or a Charlie called them later-egos. Body doubles.

I like the past in objects. In my mind, less so.

This is how a head becomes a scrapbook.

***

Who is up and who is down, who should be embraced and who should be avoided, who is all charisma and who has true talent. Greer and I talk on weekend phone dates. Mostly I dodge mention of the black dog. Jacked on coffee or Diet Coke so I have momentum for our chats, I tell her what I'm reading and watching, but not much of what I'm feeling or living, which has the low hum of sameness. Complaint is a no. Denunciation and judgment (quip with a whip) are yeses. When Greer texts on Thursday to talk on Sunday and I have hardly moved from the couch except to work two afternoon bar shifts, I grab an index card and make a list, so I have something to say. Organize your thoughts. Create conversation so when she asks how I am, I don't say, because she isn't asking, and she isn't telling. A smatter of sad goes a long way. I don't want to explain myself— or even believe it possible—or shape my life. Let others mark my achievements as flukes and my failures as true. If they even bother.

***

The radiator rattles and clangs and thick heat fills the room. I crack one of the two windows. A broken air conditioner blocks the other.

I unscrew the air conditioner from the window frame and carefully fold the dirty baffles in place. They look like crumpled moth wings. As I pull the unit out, I slip. The pain is sharp and immediate. Blood hits the air and runs down the baffles. Red sprinkles my shirt and the wall.

In the bathroom, I rinse my hand under cold water. When the bleeding lets up, I see I've sliced four fingertips. The crosshatching of cuts gives the skin the appearance of frilly flower petals. On closer inspection it looks as if I tried to destroy my finger-prints so I could slip off into a new identity, an unknown life without any connections or borders. My fingers throb— oddly reassuring.

***

I have dragged myself to the gym to swim laps and iron out my mind with a breaststroke. I interrupt a guy flexing for a selfie in the locker room but defuse any awkwardness by saying "It's hard to serve drama in a mini-dress" in my best Locust Valley lockjaw as I waltz backward out the door.

***

My beard has gone full castaway, but my barber retired and sold his business to born-again Christians. "It's now called A Shaving Grace. I shit you not," I say.

Avery suggests a beard straightener.

"Don't you see my beard is pure laziness and a way for a bald man to show a little less skin. It's about modesty and sloth."

The beard lets me hide in plain sight. Men don't fuck with me on the street, sneering as they walk directly at and into me until I move out of their way, toward the curb, toward traffic, calling faggot from cars. With my shaved head, feral beard, and unsmiling demeanor, they treat me as one of their own. Shallow cover. I appreciate the ease though my mind pulses with Valerie Solanas.

***

When I ask, "How are you doing?" what I'm saying is: "What are you thinking?" I notice when someone transgresses or makes a mistake, people often ask them, "What were you thinking?" when they mean, "Why did you do that?"

I knew what I was doing. I have always known what I was doing. Even when I was lying to myself and destroying myself, I knew what I was doing.

***

When my life imploded and I left the west coast, people were mad I'd fled. They didn't want me to understay my shunning. I'd known them in many places. Same people, same educations, same poses. Righteousness and integrity. Who could afford those? They had the money to have standards. I needed to eat.

I reconnected with Charlie around that time. I told as much of the story as I could bear. I want to believe I took the measure of the damage done and distilled it. Likely I subtracted what I could to preserve some small dignity.

I laughed because I couldn't cry. I had fucked it all up and I was never going to be forgiven, so you can imagine how hilarious it was.

"You are doomed," Charlie said.

"Dead man walking," I said.

He was laughing too but his was drier.

"So, it's going to be bad?"

"The worst that something like this can be."

"Not that you've ever been through something like this before."

"There's a first time for everything, especially last things."

A pocket of tenderness between us. Charlie wanted to know what to say but he didn't. That bothered him because like me he was rarely at a loss for words. I loved his unknowing.

***

Am I impossible? And if no, why not?

"I wouldn't say you're difficult," Charlie says. "Prickly, maybe."

"Like a porcupine."

"Like a retired actress teaching yoga in Santa Fe."

"Meow."

***

In my dream, I open my thrift store herringbone coat and show all the watches. Let you see the hustle because that's part of the hustle.

***

Some people walk like they are scouting locations for a movie, notice every detail, cataloguing, photographing. I walk like I swim, turning my mind into a line. Lately my thoughts are more like tantrums. Flustered little bullies. My life has scattered, and I can't gather it. Scraps now: matchbooks, napkins, parking tickets, credit card slips, bills past due, washing instructions, a grocery list. Not yet an eviction notice. A fragment a day keeps the ghosts away.

My little stroll: cross the bridge and head to Downer Avenue, turn right and walk until I reach the bookstore where I browse for a while, sometimes buying a book, often nothing, and continue along E. North Avenue, cross another bridge, turn north on Humboldt, and continue until I'm home again, where I place the book or nothing on the table, fetch a cigarette, and stand in the backyard smoking and examining the same tree branches as usual and thinking—or not—about writing, work, cock. I try to enjoy the walk, the cigarette (only one per day, I promise), and the branches because soon enough it will be deep winter, and I'll be bound to the apartment for months slathering my body with creams to keep my skin from cracking and fattening myself from boredom and immobility. A flaneuse walking between kitchen, living room, bedroom.

***

Me: How fragmented is too fragmented? Is there such a thing?

Greer: In art there is no such thing as too fragmented. In life, that's a different question.

Me: I'm not an artist.

***

I only have two absolutes: I will not work Friday Fish Fry or a Packers game day. But now I have violated one to sub a shift and make some extra cash. A football game is on TV at the bar. I'm mystified and repulsed until I think of the players as lesbians. Huddled, back-slapping, sisterly. Sunday belongs to dykes. I clap and cheer.

The game Charlie and I play: Who said it Buddha or William S. Burroughs? "You must learn to exist with no religion, no country, no allies. You must learn to live alone in silence."

"Buddha?'

"Burroughs."

I talk about *Gloria* starring Gena Rowlands. I often think of the scene in the cab where the kid she's saved after his family was killed by the mob says he wants to go home and Gloria tells him, "Hey, don't be stupid. You don't got no home, you got me."

"Brutal," Charlie says.

"I always think it's loving."

Charlie tells me his roommate is chasing hangovers and gonorrhea, as one does. "I don't give two splats about who he fucks, but I'm too old for it. I mean, doing it or being around it." Charlie's hints that I could move in at the end of his roommate's lease have been met with my silence. Living together would be a disaster. No matter what, being someone's tenant changes everything. And I might not be so different from his roommate. I'm chasing lost time and last chances. Gonorrhea is treatable.

***

Greer always wanted to be an artist. Charlie, a writer. I wanted to be a character actress in the 1940s, but there were many obstacles.

When someone says their art comes from some force outside of them—god, muse, the universe—I think they'll say anything to avoid responsibility.

"I hate when people compare creating art to birth" is fair statement as long as we agree calling a child a miracle is also wrong. Only a cup of coffee is a miracle.

***

I text Greer "I'm lost" and she sends back the kindest words about life and our relationship. I meant I couldn't find her new studio's building.

Greer has fallen into a funk. "I won't let people think this was all I could achieve."

I say I understand, and I do—if I imagine myself possible of success.

"I'm not sure if it's a tradition or a superstition, but after I've been through a difficult period, I throw away my clock and buy a new one," she says. "I can't wait to be on new time when this shit's over."

I want to remind Greer where she was just a few years ago. I want to say look at how fast things changed. But coming from me, what does it mean?

***

I know the story from retellings and the rest in my own way.

Once Greer realized she had mistaken masochism for perseverance, leaving was a song on continuous play. On I-5 to the airport, she watched tall pines zip by. How had life gotten so small?

In Chicago, art supplies went in storage. Greer waited for signs while she wandered strange streets. Friends sent memes, words of encouragement, and tough love. One mailed a crystal, an astrology book, and a note: *Protect your heart.*

Her sister in Milwaukee called with cancer news and Greer packed at once. Afternoons, Greer helped her niece with homework at the dining room table as Liz slept on the couch.

After chemo, Liz hurried but didn't make it, vomiting across the floor. Greer watched her sister moving about like an action painter. Liz waved her off, backing down the hallway, bent over.

Her niece decorated the Christmas tree: musty pageantry and brittle bulbs. Liz smiled through pain and Greer drank too much. Texts went unreturned.

February was suicide-watch month. Greer checked in with depressed friends and held back her own story.

March was birthy and Liz died. The niece went to the ex-husband and the house was sold. Greer found an apartment and talked about returning to Chicago or moving to Savannah.

The mattress factory shift was ten hours. One hour lunch and two fifteen-minute breaks. Greer messaged with coastal friends and longed after coworkers' cigarettes but did not partake.

She thought about Jay DeFeo painting *The Rose* for seven years. Brandy drinking, chain smoking, layering oils mixed with mica chips until the canvas weighed almost a ton and wouldn't dry. It had to be fork-lifted out the second-story bay window, ripping a piece of the wall away as it went.

Greer unpacked her paints. She would find a way to love it again. She would become obsessed and work all night like she once had. An hour later, she was in bed streaming a show people praised. It reminded her of something, but she fell asleep before she remembered what.

Her younger coworkers talked about vibes and cringe. Styles she had worn decades ago had returned. She bought a Tasmanian Devil sweatshirt at Goodwill. $4.99.

She dreamed of Liz. They'd never been close, but gone Liz was a place to visit. Greer woke damp-faced, got up, and walked the neighborhood. Familiar dogs in fenced yards put on ferocious displays.

Greer thought of a story about Agnes Martin. The older artist had hosted a young painter at her New Mexico home and issued advice. "Never have kids, never live a middle-class life, and never let anybody in your studio," Martin said, opening the door to her studio. That night, Greer dreamed about the scene. Martin was played by Liz. When she flung the studio door open, it was just a cluttered garage, and the artist told her, *Haul this shit away.*

***

Greer moves some work around. A new configuration. I say I like it and she says it's random.

Me: You mean random or random on purpose?

Greer: Random random.

4

I do understand how people disappear. How the cost of interaction is too high. When you see who is comfortable in the world, who thinks it's theirs, how can anything but disappearance be an option?

I have none of the signposts that make a life. What I do have: a former drug addiction, a history of breakdown, various disgraces, and an ability to lie in bed for long stretches of time not sleeping and not waking, not daydreaming, and not even thinking.

I have many pens with pharmaceutical companies' names on them. That can't be a good sign. What was the medication I took last year to help with bad nerves and bad sleep? Its side effects included cloudy thinking and memory loss. Was that last year?

Life is like the placards in old movies: scene missing. But I am living the lost film. Most days I am a mix of Rip Van Winkle, Jack the Ripper, and Rip Taylor: comatose, murderous, and frivolous.

I can't afford a crackup. Monetarily or emotionally. If the crash doesn't get you, the hospital bill will. And then you have to strenuously perform at life to get everyone back on your side.

No way back and no way forward. I can't get started because there are no endings. Everything loops. A strip with only its own momentum.

When the switch is on, everything's fine. When the switch is off, everything is pointless, and darkness begins dictation. Gertrude Stein's monstrosity *The Making of Americans* explains this way of existing: "Resisting being is one way of being."

***

Avery suggests an energy worker. If I had all my negative energy cleared, there'd only be bones and gristle left. Greer says depression is the mind selecting what feeds the sadness. I ask her if I stop thinking of myself as part of the world, will I let go of taking any of it personally. It's hard to take anything personally when you don't feel like a person. Only a scrap heap of mistakes and mismatched genetics with a beard spirit gummed on it.

***

People who don't get self-deprecating humor and try to reassure you are the luckiest people in the world. They don't understand when I say I'm a piece of shit, I mean they are pieces of shit too. I'm using myself as the stool sample for humanity.

Who still gets me? It's a one-handed count.

Far-flung friends have taken a turn for the worse. One who has gone life coach cuckoo sends a video on forgiveness. When it ends, I revise my shit list, adding his name. Another is a full-on crackpot spouting paranoid rambles like Dr. Bronner's All-One Pure-Castile Liquid soap packaging. Substitute 9/11, Rothschilds, psyops, and germ warfare for New Age propagandist gusto.

I have discarded several circles of friends and been discarded by others. I know or can imagine why. Necessity, survival instinct, prickly injustices, accumulated grievances. I had my reasons too. I discarded people who stopped believing my lies and people who accepted my truths. My lies: How could you not want these beautiful things I made for you? My truths: How could you want so little from me?

Are these relationships like vivisection, pointlessly confirming what I already know?

***

I dream I end up in a small cottage by a lake with a dog I walk twice a day and that lounges with me. It isn't a dream though. I am wishing for this. "Wish in one hand, shit in the other, and see which gets full faster," as my ex used to say. Vivid but unhelpful.

***

Low-rent Tiresias: I can't find my glasses and am making pronouncements.

I eat up stories of under-the-radar to hard-won to over-the-top. If they end in freefall, better still. Triumph is suspect. Disaster too predictable. Fade-outs or freeze-frames, yes and yes. Inscribing, reencountering, going over again. I repeat the stories, memorize the best lines, and discard the rest as waste.

The past comes back as startling as dreams, with the same logic. These memories aren't like stories I've made harmless or turned into utilities by repetition. They aren't comforting, which is how I know they're true.

The present is a problem. Time ellipses. Days are long and sputtery, then a month is gone. The cast-off VFW calendar with its illustrations of birds and oddly sourced inspirational quotes (Andre Gide?) flips—robin, warbler, hummingbird, tanager, grosbeaks, waxwing, chickadee—and a year is over. I must have had a life in those months, but I don't recall.

***

"Have you tried mindfulness?" Dustin says.

Why would I meditate when I've reached peak dissociation?

What the hell. I give it a shot.

"Stop talking to yourself," intones the voice of the guided meditation.

"Make a mental note of that," I whisper to myself.

"Renounce the renouncer. Destroy the destroyer."

But in renouncing the renouncer and destroying the destroyer aren't we the renouncer and the destroyer?

"Imagine looking down on your physical self."

Always.

***

Try gratitude.

Dear Black Dog, I would like to take a moment to applaud you for sticking by me all these years and for being adaptive to whatever changes I make. You truly are my most steadfast companion, and I thank but do not love you.

***

The moment you accept what you fear will never happen, and neither will what you hope for, then the next moment when you try to arrange those thoughts into something like wisdom instead of despair.

***

Avery recommends a podcast. The chatty host says there is nothing to overcome, nothing to remedy or solve. There is alongside. Living alongside. Living. How lovely. Where do I find these drugs?

***

"Captures a world irrevocably lost," says the book jacket copy, and no thank you. I have my own sunken times, but no one wants to capture them. They hardly wanted them the first go-round.

Instead, I read a hefty biography that drags until I hit short passages of gossip about a time of revered poets and poems recited aloud. Today is dumb and quiet and the term living memory betrays both words.

Greer says the things we love were always loved by few, but the population has grown, and the minds haven't. I guess Greer needs light. Artists do.

***

Charlie has a trove of old art magazines including *High Performance*. One features Jerry Dreva, a queer Milwaukee conceptual and correspondence artist. In his interview he says, "I am interested in mythologizing the mundane." He goes on to say he makes art to survive, in order to make sense of his life, to give significance and confer meaning upon it. "My art is my life. My art is a celebration of my life which I am presenting as a continual performance."

Some people believe art is whatever you do to be alive. I'm keen on the idea of life being art, but not the life we live and not the life we make. Another life. The shadow one we can't see, and it grows and shrinks as we move.

***

I'm drawn to all those anticapitalist, anticommodification 70s performance artists whose work lives on only as a few photographs, remnants of sets, moldering costumes, maybe a grainy video with dubious sound. Undocumented is unthinkable now. I have a religious feeling about those performance artists who had an audience of six as they crawled across the floor of a loft with no cameras. It's like deep balm this topic.

I pour over what remains of Stephen Varble, the Kentucky-born alien, who said his family wanted him to be a missionary. Instead, he said, he became a monster. His elaborate costumes were worn in performance protests outside museums. One with a wire-sculpture cage surrounding him with money attached to it like tissue paper flowers decorating a float. Eventually he retreated from public performance and worked on an epic, never-completed video called *Journey to the Sun*. After his death in '84 and two years later his lover's, most of Varble's possessions and work were thrown out on the street. "I'd like my costumes preserved in igloos, as opposed to pyramids," he said. "I'm afraid of dust, you see." In photos he's some strange combination of Victorian bride, Cockette, and shaman.

***

What do people do when they vanish from the world? Greer has a friend, an artist, who went from a satanic to a static life. Debauched city to pokey town. Deep quiet. Pitch-black nights with occasional supply runs for chips, cigarettes, and diet soda. He told Greer his new kink is watching the sky and distinguishing between the prophetic pathetic and the pathetic prophetic.

***

In Buddhism the self is an illusion. Perhaps true, but I've worked hard to conjure this particular sleight of hand. Most people who talk about authenticity have merely figured out how to arrange their damage into a reasonably consistent human performance. Find yourself? That's forty years in the desert and for what? I don't want to trek all that way only to discover a cliff or a frozen border.

***

In 1974 when the singer Connie Converse packed her Volkswagen Beetle and drove off never to be heard from again, she left goodbye letters. In one she wrote, "Let me go, let me be if I can, let me not be if I can't."

***

When Tuesday Weld was asked by a reporter what drove her into seclusion in the 1970s, she responded, "I think it was a Buick."

My urge is escape or to at least reclaim my mind from the world, to slow my attention, put my phone in a drawer, read a book in bed uninterrupted. Let the day and its malcontents run wild, unknown. Alone and forsaken is my heaven.

***

Release. Escape artists fascinated me as a kid. Take your pick: handcuffs, straitjackets, bags, coffins, cages, chains, steel boxes, barrels, burning buildings, fish tanks. I read about Houdini and illusionists and vanishments. D.B. Cooper, the name the FBI gave the unknown man, who hijacked a plane, demanded a ransom, and parachuted into the night over southwestern Washington state. Never identified or apprehended. I went to the public library and read about him, parachute stunts, night jumps, and canopy collisions. What I wanted to know was how to go unfound.

***

Forty individual muscles in the human face and my frown lines are the strongest. I know it doesn't help to think if certain people weren't dead the world would be more companionable, even—especially—if it is also true.

Charlie tells a story about Sam, our friend who died twenty-plus years ago, and his eyes get teary.

"Okay, let's get a drink," I say.

"I'm skint."

"I'll spot you. C'mon."

"I don't want you buying me drinks. I should be buying you drinks."

"Is this a top/bottom chivalry thing? Get your fucking coat."

***

Afterward soused Charlie sleeps on my couch. I remove his shoes and carefully lay a blanket over him. On the porch I smoke, angled to watch both the intersection where traffic whizzes along and inside where Charlie doesn't stir. Jesus Christ, it's cold.

5

Misery loves company but misery can't host.

    Grindr profile: "Nasty brutish and short."

    (Double taps)

***

Midnight, outside a bar, guts thick with bad beer, the young man in cowboy boots and I wait at the hot dog stand to create more regret. We discuss discipline that looks like punishment, solitude that looks like withdrawal, renunciation that looks like starvation. I tell him about someone who disappeared for a year, and I hardly noticed. Another friend didn't text for two days, and I panicked at what I had done or said to merit silence. We stand and shuffle our feet. Is he coming home with me? Is that what is happening? His phone lights up. He looks at the light, smiles, and says, "I should get going."

***

Avery has been on a string of bad dates.

"Big dude but he opened his mouth and a purse fell out," he says.

"Was it a 70s cigarette purse with Suzanne Pleshette's beaded likeness? If so, he's mine."

***

Charlie says his ex is dating a trophy twink. "He's fucking a twenty-year-old and I'm pushing sixty and my life is either being ghosted or invoiced. Maybe I'll invoice the ghosters and ghost the invoicers."

***

"I thought we would be Claude Cahun and Marcel Moore," Greer said of her last "big" girlfriend ten years ago. "Minus Nazis and prison of course."

"Just the artistry and hint of incest?"

"Just a whiff."

***

Hugh texts he will be in town Friday and Saturday. Pick a night.

Saturday. Not that it matters. I have no plans.

He sends his hotel information.

Can't wait to see you, I type, then delete. See you Saturday, I send. The text equivalent of butching it up. Idiotic.

We start with drinks at the hotel bar. For a few hours I am in the bubble, and back at the hotel in a room larger than my apartment on expensive sheets, sadness broadsides me. I make my fear into motion and put it on his body. Afterward, I lie on top of him, and he says, "That was intense." I run my hand through his hair, along his forehead, and gently close his eyelids.

***

The sign on the door reads DO YOU KNOW WHO YOU ARE LETTING IN?

A good precautionary reminder that can quickly turn into an existential whirlpool.

***

Charlie suggests online dating though both of us have had terrible results.

Turn-ons: 1970s and 1980s Performance art, Fluxus, No Wave music, New Narrative writing, New

York School poetry, Boston School photographers, queer-core, punk drag queens, cult actresses, ghost-writers, appropriation, Oulipo, Nouveau Roman, unfinished work, notebooks, journals, dairies, and fragments.

Turn-offs: Everything else.

***

Me, flirting: "This is back in the 90s when you'd write your rent check in red ink to buy yourself an extra day in bank processing."

***

Sometimes I miss when people lied to each other in person. You go along to get along until you are gone. There are no prizes for guessing at answers to questions that lack conviction.

***

Avery tells me his friend I'd expressed interest in described me as a bilious misanthropist— flattery will get you everywhere—and a negationist. That's a lot of -ists.

"Okay," I say, "but does he want to fuck?"

***

Filling out a health history I skip the Single / Married / Divorced / Widowed line and the desk says you forgot one. No, that was intentional. I'm none of those things.

Hookup apps have warped me. In the examination room, I have to give my age, height, and weight and I expect the nurse to say, "I only like muscle bear bottoms."

***

I want to bring a stranger here, make him face the wall, and fuck him. I want him to be much larger than me and have my face somewhere in the region of his shoulder blades. He could physically over-power me, but he won't. We have strict roles.

***

"I like older guys" (Check)
"I like short guys" (Check)
"I like funny guys" (I have jokes)
"I like rich guys" (Bye)

***

I go to a man's place and post fuck he tells me, "I always knew I was special." I dress in record time.

***

"It felt like such a bad idea that I decided to go with it," Avery says.

"Is a hard cock an idea?"

"Better than many."

Avery talks about a man he was infatuated with and chased for a year. More balls than sense. Patience of a hand grenade. Like most bullies, the guy believed himself a truthteller. Another punisher in love with his own tongue. Avery says the man talked constantly about his sense of duty and his strong bonds, his courtesy visits and check-ins. All lurking to find those made to hurt and gather ways to do it. Absolutely controlling and would anger if Avery didn't support him in everything he said. Finally, Avery's loyalty faltered when the guy's sanity vacationed in deep paranoia. He wrote Avery a scathing accusatory novella-length goodbye text.

"Nightmare," I say.

Avery says, "I miss him."

***

Under the covers with my laptop beside me, I'm distractedly perusing porn. A video is titled *Farewell Fuck*. A comment underneath says, "So hot. Why goodbye?"

I skip to titles like *Rocco and Max*, *Young Fucks Bear*, *My Sexy Daddy*, and the familiar roulette of my spank bank. I search for specific images and positions. Similar type men: older—my age. Thicker middles, hairy, bearded, graying, balding, balder, baldest.

Cartoon machine gun fire and laughter bleed in from the apartment next door.

***

Is it an Afghan proverb or the Talmud or some goddamn meme that says not word, not actions, but patterns are where the true expression of who we are lies? My exhaustion is I have performed these same acts again and again, and I do them because they are all I have.

***

Dustin worked third shift. He texts, "I spent half the night wandering around the hotel in my slippers and a hoodie. Stole a fifteen-dollar slice of cake and watched YouTube on my phone in the ballroom surrounded by Irish linen wall coverings and silk-shaded chandeliers. I was almost passed out tired the entire time. Now I'm home and I can't sleep. Come over."

***

On the couch pressed against Dustin. He reaches down lazily and knocks over his beer. Shit. Angie immediately laps at the spill. I get up, walk naked across the apartment, and grab a dishrag and a beer. Glance at the refrigerator photos of Dustin and his husband at the beach, on a road trip, at a cabin.

Dustin blots at the rug. "Fuck." He abandons the spot. Angie nabs the rag, and we laugh as she runs across the room. We lie back down on the couch. I want to fall asleep beside him, my face against his neck smelling his hair, my arm over him, my hand on the curve of his belly, my cock against his ass.

"I have to go soon," I say.

Dustin mumbles as I remove myself from his warmth. Rag abandoned, Angie wags her tail in anticipation of going out and circles while I dress. I lean over the couch and kiss his sleeping face. On my way down the creaking stairs, I hear someone on the porch and stand motionless, awaiting the opening door and the husband. Then the neighbor's voice thanks a delivery person and footsteps trail off. I hustle outside onto the sidewalk, shaky and turned-on.

6

Sometimes I try to remember my past lives. They weren't good times, but they weren't this. I imagine some different words or actions to undo the present. A cocaine-couraged disaster night is reversed, the straw rewound, the fat line reappearing. A job quit is surfed out a little longer until the monkey bar of another appears and a terrible apartment with a worse man is never moved into. I can do this all night and I do.

***

I always imagined the devil was a fast talker, but the devil spoke slow.

We went to the ocean because it was free. I was in the blast radius of my disgrace, and he was pin-balling between rebounds. I didn't want to talk about what had nearly killed me. I'd quit smoking so I didn't know what to do with my hands. He said the last guy shot like a cartoon star. Gestured big. The tide dribbled up comically before us. The whole wide world at my back. The air and water cold. *You can lead a whore to water.* He walked right up like he was ordering a drink.

Swagger and affinity. The joint was his. He brought up long-ago stories meant to embarrass me, and I remembered who he was and always would be. Who needed rivals or idols when the world was friendless?

***

My boyfriend was sleeping with my friend and when they were discovered, I asked if they were in love. He said yes. Who was I to stand in the way of love? Who was I?

***

Gloria Swanson on a sitcom starring Wayland Flowers and Madame, 1980:

Gloria: How many husbands have you had?

Madame: How many? I've had six husbands of my own and four of my friends.

***

A decade ago, my on-again/off-again boyfriend traveled out west and sent postcards from places with names like Deception Pass and Romantic Bluff. I didn't take the hint.

Each afternoon I checked the mailbox hoping for word from him. I usually found disappointment: junk mail, forwarded magazine subscriptions, bills, and legal notices. I dutifully placed them in the recycling bin.

Occasionally a postcard came. A different type of disappointment. He said little. A capsule description of a landscape, a list of images, a skinny poem, no salutation, no sign-off, only his initial: B.

I was staying with a friend. My life was a wreck—underemployed, terrible credit, deeply depressed—and hers wasn't much better. We watched movies together and took turns running to the bodega to buy mac n' cheese, canned soup, and alcohol. Miraculously according to some, weirdly according to me, her fortunes improved. My presence became vaguely embarrassing.

Summer came. She was back to normal: working, running errands, and joining friends for beers. Bored and lonely, I stayed in the house, ordered things I didn't need online, and sent flurries of text messages to busy friends. Slumped at my computer, I looked at acquaintances' vacation photos and read their gripes and boasts.

I knew I'd hit an impasse and needed to *move forward* as people on TV and in books with long subtitles were constantly evangelizing, but I no longer held certainty about the concept of progress. Velocity? Sure. Entropy? Absolutely. I could believe in speed and decay.

B was quiet. Last I'd heard, he was in Boulder, Colorado.

Long ago, I'd stayed with my aunt outside Aspen where she lived in a roadside motel that had been refurbished and turned into apartments. On our family visit, my mother had declared she needed a break from me, and her sister offered for me to stay the summer. I watched television late into the night and slept while my aunt was at work in the local hospital's laundry. I picked up poetry chapbooks at a dusty store and punk albums a few doors down in a cramped room mottled with band stickers and defiant faces on posters. At night, we rode around in my aunt's bright red truck and shared joints. I didn't want to return to my mother and dreamed of leaving and being out on my own. A year later I would be, and it wouldn't be anything like those months.

I wanted to tell B all of that, but he hated the phone.

In July, a postcard arrived with a poem:

clouds
nothing at all
songbirds
& a stone
rolls away

I surveyed the clothes strewn on the floor, kitchen mess, neglected bills, empties, and my phone where my life had reduced to a series of digital communications, many one-sided.

Upstairs, I pulled all of B's postcards from a drawer and tore them into a scramble of broken phrases. My mouth tasted sour. I threw the scraps in the bathroom trash can and caught my frantic reflection in the mirror. Make a plan. It would involve phone calls with a bright and casual tone of voice, a bus or plane ticket, and the nagging idea I might see my frantic face again in another mirror in another place. My only certainty: leave no forwarding address.

***

The blue gate was open. His bicycle was gone. I brushed leaves off a chair in the yard and waited. Dogs of all sizes passed, curious, indifferent, yaps and barks and wagging. A book I was struggling to finish in hand. I heard a bicycle and turned happily. Not him. A scowling old man. I left the book on the chair.

***

My grimy valentine: him, infatuated, and them, slim-hipped skater-model types, greasy-haired, blankish. He photographed them and years later rephotographed the photos. Skinny-boy bodies as ready-mades, Duchamp's *Fountain* walking down the street in Venice Beach.

***

Wiper blades smeared the lights. I lifted my head off the seat-back and saw the car ahead, imagined if we drifted into it. Not fast but with a crunch of metal and breaking glass. My head slumped back. When I opened my eyes, we had pulled to a stop.

The man led the way. I stood at the foot of the stairs, trying to figure out what I was doing, wavering.

His pull extinguished my will, and I followed him up. I trailed my hand along the wall.

He rambled on and told me, "Don't let anyone into your life just because you're lonely." I couldn't help but laugh.

He told me, "I'm a drunk and I can't be faithful." I spent the next year not seeing his central declaration as fact, treating it as a hypothesis to disprove. He wasn't loyal but he hated change.

What I liked about him: His family had passed a decree of damnatio memoriae against him. We went to St. Mary's Cemetery in Appleton, Wisconsin and he pissed on Joe McCarthy's grave. He made soups: congee, posole, minestrone, red lentil, and bulgur. I'd never eaten soup that wasn't from a can or a restaurant. He said, "There's a sucker born every minute, but most of them aren't good at it."

Sometimes he was like a man boarding a train. Moving but not awake. Small in the morning. Other mornings my face had been tenderized and I didn't remember the exact sequence of events that had led up to it. We would start yelling but we were numbed on drugs and fighting was like a dance. I broke a few plates to get his attention. They were beautiful scattered on the floor.

His idea of kindness: he said I was great at anticipating people's needs. Maybe he wanted a butler, not a boyfriend. Maybe I would have made a great footman. Or foot stool.

My throat was sore inside and out, from yelling and being choked. I held my broken glasses. The room was fuzzy. In the bathroom, I saw blood on my ear. I wiped it off and watched where the red dot returned. A nick on the top. I went to the closet and put on my snow boots, left the laces undone. Checked the floor for glass and saw drips of blood. Followed their crooked trail up the wall to the mirror which had one crack snaking along the lower left side.

I could take the hits and the other men but not the silence. I took a year to realize he loved his pain more than anything else, especially me. We settled into routine. Or a truce. I looked for common ground. Like how we both hated me. I practiced leaving many nights as something broke in the kitchen and I pretended to sleep. He came to bed drunk and put his arm around me. He readjusted the covers and withdrew, turned away, exposing his scratched-up back. I looked at the expense and thought of dirt falling across it.

***

When will I be good enough for you? By the time I could form the question, I already knew the answer.

***

Twenty years ago, dancing and sweating in a crowd, then going home alone because I was too afraid of rejection and bless that dumb little fool.

Some nights I went to the Eagle to make out in a corner with some eager dude down from Everett for the night. Hands a little too grabby, mouth a little too hard. I was off work and off drugs, so time was measured by a stiff cock in denim rubbed against me to three-and four-minute songs. Walk out to a parked car for head and back in time for the aging DJ to play the original "Tainted Love" sung by Gloria Jones or the epic stretch of joy "I (Who Have Nothing)" by Sylvester and I was transported to some other era, away from Seattle's drizzle and defeat.

***

Not love. Lust, maybe, or recognition. I lived in the moment and the moment was wherever my hand landed. First, a glass. As the night got darker, a flirty stranger's thigh. He sat on a barstool turned out, legs spread wide. The type of boyish good looks I wanted to smear across a pillow. His name, his occupation, and his opinions did not matter. Blank men. That was where you wrote the sex.

***

The apartment smelled dank. One room. Clothes covered the floor. He knocked a few things from a table. The bed was pushed against the far wall.

Dishes and glasses were piled in the sink. He rinsed two tumblers and filled them. He grinned and kissed me hard. Pressed against me, mouth to my ear. He stripped off his shirt. His body was mostly good with a little bit of flesh like a deflated balloon and some marks along his abdomen. I swung between excitement and irritation. We moved like parts of a composite: jerking, baring, concealing.

Absence dug in and dragged me to other places. I thought of other men. An electrical charge returned, and I was lost in a rhythm, trying to not let my mind slow down.

He panted and whimpered, and his face twisted, and he said someone's name between clenched teeth.

He stood unsteadily and walked to the bathroom. I cleaned myself with rough tissues from a box by the bed. I was still hard, at half-mast, ridiculous.

I closed my eyes against the brightness and lay back in the snarl of sheets. He returned and pressed his wilted cock against me. I wasn't in the bed. I was far away with a warm body left behind like family you sent a little money back to each month with a note: *How is grandma? America is great.*

He mumbled something. I fetched more whiskey and returned to his snoring body jackknifed across the mattress. Picked through the clothes and found mine. His wallet was on the floor, and I opened it. Seventy-two bucks. I took forty.

***

I met him day-drinking in a pool hall after work. Calculated worker dude affect to throw people off the lisp and the way he walked on the balls of his steel-toed boots. I wore jeans with burn marks from cigarettes, a sloppy thrift store suit jacket over a torn tee, and faggy shoes with Cuban heels. Bedhead Truffaut street allure. He talked to me but avoided eye contact. After I took him for some cash, he paid attention. We went to my place because my roommates didn't care if I stumbled in at four in the afternoon with a stranger. He was fun—a big body, fat, and ripe smelling. I'd been living on crackers and booze and cigarettes so someone spilling over in my hands was hot. Holding his tits up to my teeth, parting that huge ass, two ridiculous slopes spilling over. We tasted of smoke and fried food and poor hygiene. His sweetness and sadness were the thing I clung to all winter and spring. Meeting up in the afternoons, going to my place. Never his, never hanging out at night, never in fag bars. Only daylight and drunk. Then as I always did, I had to leave. A seasonal runaway with the promise of a rooftop tar paper beach summers. We weren't anything but I knew I'd miss him, and I liked to think he'd miss me.

***

"If you could change one thing—"

"One thing? You flatter me."

Late night, we were both tired and I was leaving town in the morning. What we'd had was gone but we wanted to linger in the goneness. We knew lingering was a mistake. When I left, I wasn't returning. My possessions were gone. Nothing kept me there except the moment of trying to pinpoint one regret, one thing to change. That process of elimination could take a lifetime.

My glass was empty. "I should go. I'm fading."

He stood with some effort. I moved toward the door, and he followed. I turned to touch him but that would only postpone what was next. Intimacy stalled the future. "Night."

***

Russ Terrible said life was love. Love was all there was. He was in love when he said it.

"I like taking care of someone," Russ said.

He kicked his lover out and cleaned up. Took the lover back. They started using again. Lover fucked around. Kicked lover out again. Took lover back again.

"I missed looking after him."

Next I heard, Russ was alone, had lost his money, home, and job. He was clean.

"That's good, "I said.

"That motherfucker will pay," he said.

I nodded, but I knew better. Motherfuckers never pay. Motherfuckers take. If they give, it's with their cocks. Only us mothers get fucked.

***

Two months after we broke up, Leo asked me to meet for a drink.

"You look good," I said. Instant regret.

He glowed. I was gray in proximity to his vigor. Falling out of love with me suited him. Then it hit me: He was in love with someone new. Hadn't he been seeing someone right before me? Hadn't he made it clear he was incapable of being solitary?

Our meeting was a house call. I was foolish to have expected anything else. Leo didn't want to be an asshole and he was having drinks with me to prove he wasn't.

I told him the most palatable version of my life I could muster. The conversation reminded me of Dr. Seuss or Gertrude Stein's *Business in Baltimore*: "yes and more and yes and yes and why." We were saying plenty and yet saying nothing. I knew I'd made a mistake in accepting the invitation, and Leo was probably having the same awareness.

The strange sense of time repeating. All the moments I'd waited for something obvious to be said: an apology. That wouldn't happen but the yearning for an apology had replaced lust. A show of decency was unattainable.

We finished and loitered on the sidewalk, both shuffling. I was animated and twice I caught Leo watching my hands. Shiny-eyed with drink, he clapped my shoulder. We parted and I didn't turn back.

7

Note to self: You can stay in bed all day but that doesn't make you Colette.

***

I hate the sensation: an instinctive gutter ball. I'm mad this is the default.

Turn my phone off, hole up at home, watch old movies. No laundry because I don't change clothes. Dishes pile up. Apples brown on the kitchen counter and smell of sweet rot.

Undependable. I call around to find subs for my bar shifts and turn down catering gigs, knowing I'll be broke. I lie on the bed with an unread and unreadable book and watch snow diagonal past my window.

The hum overtakes me, my chest tightens, and a flutter of uncalm grows. Greer once told me a thing to do. Locate five orange things (or whatever color) in your immediate environment. The search and count refocus and interrupt the alarm. I do orange, red, blue, yellow, green. Black, I can count until dawn.

***

Greer says, "One panic attack and these kids think they're a combination of Sylvia Plath and a war veteran." I picture her fiddling with her amber necklace—a gift from a former mentor or an ex-girlfriend (both) she mentions around the end of December every year or so.

***

Sometimes the chase is too convoluted, strange, errant, and ongoing, there is no way to cut to it.

The phone brings questions and the quest-ions either don't have answers or have the wrong answers which bring more questions. Before long I have fallen mute and there are expressions of concern. The messages address me gently as if I am lost and they can bring me back, when it is precisely these words that have silenced me.

My fallback comfort: Things are built to change, by which I mean to fall apart. Not only of the individual but of the idea, society, everything visible and knowable and unknowable. When entropy is a comfort you know you're fucked.

Avery has called me a cynic. I'm pessimistic by nature but I wouldn't say I'm cynical. If I were cynical, I'd be making money. Cynics get rich. Pessimists stay poor.

**

I only see the dark currents around the room, the glances between people, the little aggressions, the distortions, and I miss the rest. The details I need to survive are the foreground and much of what others might deem important is wallpaper. It is helpful for tending bar.

The music at work is loud tonight. I misheard "karmic" as "comic" and have been agreeing to all kinds of nonsense. Occasionally a sharp goose honk cuts through the noise. The repressed anger in Wisconsin bleeds out in those sharply nasal vowels. "My aunt always said the devil's like a dog on a chain: if you don't go near him, he can't bite you. I like dogs though."

A man is into a well-worn tale. He's told this story for laughs, and he's told this story for pity. He doesn't remember what happened. Or he wishes he didn't.

"It goes without saying," he says.

I have inadvertently spiritually murdered a regular by saying, "If the song was popular when we were in our twenties it's an oldie." When I see the look on her face (she's had work done so it takes some discernment), I want to rescind my words. I forget my embrace of obsolescence isn't shared.

A redhead in a Packer jersey drops a pitcher of beer. Gold and glass explode, and he swears loudly. Outside a woman pushing a stroller through snow with Sisyphean determination glares as a cry goes up from the baby covered with a blanket like a parakeet. Two drunks chicken dance, puff up for a fight, swing wild and wide. A constabulary of bystanders murmur keep the peace. It is unkept. The men shimmy rubber-legged into the street and across to a vacant lot. Not my problem.

***

Who said when I die build me a funeral pyre of all the books I never read?

I spent the day organizing mine, unread, read, forgotten, still haunted. Most acquired from used bookstores and estate sales. My first summer catering weddings I bought back the Nan Goldin monographs I'd hocked for heroin.

"Sickness you wouldn't wish on the devil himself," Charlie says. The depravity of addiction: I sold my library.

A former friend's poetry is on my shelf. Each chapbook was dedicated to a new lover. Seven books, seven lovers. Each dedicatee the One at the time. Until death do us. There are a lot of ways to die without dying.

The way to do a book dedication: *To all those I've lied to.*

***

The poetry I love is the poetry people say isn't poetry. It's usually the universal things I don't relate to at all. Any honest description of survival isn't inspirational, it's frightening.

***

I went to a poetry reading where Victor Hugo's quote that "An intelligent hell would be better than a stupid paradise" was disproven. All the poets read off their phones. It was like being ignored at a party.

***

Pretty sure I attributed something to *The Book of Disquiet* by Fernando Pessoa that may have been said to me by a bartender/coke dealer at Jocko's Rocket Ship in Madison, Wisconsin, circa 1992. I go to Merriam-Webster online and listen to the pronunciation of philistine again and again and again until I am satisfied.

***

I lent Dustin a favorite novel.

"Where's the redemption?" he says.

Dustin wants hope. For me redemption is not giving up. Perseverance is too fancy a word. Getting through. Isn't it enough to still be alive and more or less intact? I consider that astonishing. Not dead, not dead inside, still moving. Still on the bus at five in the morning on the way to a temp job and the bus driver talks about how difficult getting off the toilet is with two knee replacements. I believe him. I say, "I bet."

***

I want to read books with narrators who are middle-aged but not the middle-aged we usually encounter in novels where they assess their lives after divorce or illness or have a mid-life crisis. I want artistically inclined but thwarted working-class queer people trying to make rent, trying to pay bills, trying to find reasons to keep going. They want love and freedom but are suspicious of both words because they have witnessed how they have been twisted to mean their opposites.

***

Reading about writers *discovered* after their deaths: "Ignored during her lifetime..." Now that you're dead and the messiness of your human presence and existence has been extinguished, let us praise you and reprint your work.

In his introduction to Alejandra Pizarnik's poetry collection, Enrique Vila-Matas writes, "I say this to whoever wants to listen: when we believe we can see life and work fusing in the figure of a writer, let us consider that their life is deliberately false and has been invented solely to support the work, which truly is real."

Charlie once told me he started writing so it looked to others and even himself like he was busy. If he had a vocation than being home alone was no one's business.

An editor once asked him, "Who is your audience?"

He said smart, damaged people with a lot of feelings.

Charlie's revision process: Pare down a short piece into one paragraph. Expand with new material. Cut new material. Cut more until one good line remains. Write it on the wall in light pencil. Forget it.

***

My true vocation: lying on the floor listening to music.

From Joni Mitchell's liner notes to the album *Mingus*: "Charles Mingus, a musical mystic, died in Mexico, January 5, 1979, at the age of 56. He was cremated the next day. That same day 56 sperm whales beached themselves on the Mexican coastline and were removed by fire. These are the coincidences that thrill my imagination."

I play jazz and Nico, the sounds of heroin. Before Nico gets to moan the chorus of David Bowie's "Heroes" —*And we can be herrroooeees just for one day* —

by way of introduction, she asks the fervently applauding audience "Why do you give me so much gratitude?" Indeed.

***

I remember sitting on the back porch sipping coffee after being out drinking all night wondering if I'd ever get old and being young would be a memory. I was listening to the song I'm listening to now.

***

Aretha Franklin's cover of "Eleanor Rigby" is energized, not a ballad, not triumphant but maybe defiant. She changes the lyrics from third to first person, singing, *I'm Eleanor Rigby*. Right away, transformed. It reminds me of a radio interview with Janet Frame. Asked about writing memoirs, she says, "That is the desire, really, to make myself a first-person. For many years I was a third-person." Her voice is small and polite. When the interview existed on YouTube it was a black screen. No images. Only Frame's voice in the dark.

***

"This is a new song I wrote." Each song is introduced in a drawl. Her singing is brackish. It's been a long tour, a longer life. Acclaim and attention didn't come until she was well into her forties, an age near death in popular culture. For a few years—maybe it was someone's advice, maybe it was her own choice—she tried to femme it up with soft makeup and gentle cascading hairstyles that were lighter and blonder every time I saw her. Tonight, she looks like hell but smiles between songs, sometimes during. It's not the shy glimmer from when she was starting out. It's inscrutable, a private ricochet that hits the corners of her mouth and her eyes. Lost in the songs, moved by the ache in her voice, the impossibility of loving or being loved in the right ways—in all the ways we imagine that don't exist.

Afterward Avery says, "Great songs, wrong dress."

***

I need to think of my life like a touring band and remember the musician's creed: Don't let civilians on the bus.

***

Charlie can't go to shows now. His ears can't take it. I remember our last one. Sound seared the small space. A sweat box of roiling bodies kept cell phones tucked away. Too much chaos and pushing to risk damage. I didn't want to be the old guy excited by the raucous crowd, the din, narrowing his eyes and seeing the room like one from two decades ago filled with friends and acquaintances but I was. The wave washed over me with the rising roar of the band. The singer half-crouched, stalked her small piece of the stage, snarled, and spit. My god.

Afterward we stopped for a slice next door and the guys at the next table debated who invented punk. A man outside walked up and vomited on the window. True punk.

Maybe one reason I like female-fronted punk bands is my mother was a yeller. Gives me a homey feeling. The anger of my old punk albums is still fresh. This fearful rage sung in wild harmonies with sped-up rockabilly guitar riffs is about careening drunk through disappointment and sadness as time slips away, leaving something half-healed and half-wounded. The singer keens, *A life of intermission, a life of intermission...*

Punk, the great destroyer that refused to die, and hauls out its Madame Tussaud's forty-year anniversary tours. The singing sourer, the iffy nihilism taken a reactionary veer into crackpot theories of false flag school shootings.

I'm in the mood for some cartoon nihilism. I have a Teenage Jesus and the Jerks record around here unless I sold it. Every other year, I decide something—a record, a book, a sweater—is heavy with bad memories and sell it. Making room for good. Inevitably I crave a song or a story or the comfort of the worn sweater and they aren't there. I lived on this record and ramen for a winter. The scrape and dissonance ripped at the air. *Roach bomb music. Put on a platter and watch them scatter.* Here it is. Now to be pummelled.

8

Charlie and I talk about acquaintances flying off to destination weddings and circuit parties. How men scoff at using condoms because they're on PrEP and antibiotic resistant gonorrhea, syphilis, and chlamydia rates are soaring. We both hate it all but what else can we do? Even a hermit needs to get dicked down sometimes.

After Leo dumped me, I told Greer I was back on the market, and she said you are not a commodity. But we all are. This world treats us all as whores and then we spend our social lives convincing ourselves someone else is a dirtier, nastier whore than us. Respectability politics is not rimming dirty assholes for fun, I guess.

I don't understand the world now. I feel like a faggotus rex. But the truth is I didn't understand the world back then either.

***

I crave an old encounter. The feeling when you run into someone you haven't seen in a long time, and you realize it's an affront to them you no longer carry yourself like you are ashamed to be alive. I want to be him again.

***

Charlie shows me old copies of the AIDS zine *Diseased Pariah News*. We flip through them. Pitch black humor by people with AIDS for people with AIDS. It upset pieties, including my own. There was a New Age push during the height of the AIDS epidemic to heal by loving yourself. The implication being you'd gotten sick by not loving yourself. Loving and healing and letting go. All that rot. Derek Jarman talked about being encouraged to use Buddhist detachment from pain: "Gautama Buddha instructs me to walk away from illness, but he wasn't attached to a drip... we all contemplated suicide."

The period was suffused with sickness, and not just illness, but the immorality of politicians, preachers, and healers. That took a dark toll and damaged those of us who witnessed it. How do you heal after that? Many had to forget, to bury their friends and their feelings. The rage was too much. Others rode it out, but it wore them down. Some withdrew. Some became scolds, mouthpieces, experts. Some turned to drugs. Ron Athey said, "Is healing being restored to what you were when you were twenty-three? Or is healing becoming a kind of monster on the other side who survived?" You can't go backward and be restored. You must be a monster. There's something of the harridan's laugh having come out the other side. You're scarred but alive. I think of Marianne Faithfull describing her voice as "loaded with time." What can you do but sing?

***

I remember the list of afflictions, the suffering. All the queens dying. Regicide. And then I would work as many shifts as I could until I had money. I saved to spend it all on a ticket somewhere else, to start over. As if death wouldn't follow.

***

In an interview, the writer is asked about a story in which the narrator "wonders whether there is a way of being selfish without hurting anyone." She responds, "By never marrying, and living alone and having long conversations in the middle of the night with a friend. And by never seeing that person." I have done all of these and no dice. I still hurt people. And I guess I was one of those hurt too.

***

The ocean, Charlie says is the only thing louder than his tinnitus. He misses it. Lake Michigan doesn't work. We went to the Atlantic with Sam once.

A photo I still have—even after all these moves and the eviction when the super threw my possessions into the trash: Sam's back to the camera, head up, watching something move in the sky. Or maybe nothing.

As a kid, Sam told me, he'd bought a telescope with money from summers he worked corn detasseling. He talked about comets, supernovae, variable stars, double stars, sunspots, asteroids, and occultations of stars by the moon. Young stellar events, he began. That's us, I joked. Space excited him and his usual clipped demeanor slipped as his spoke. His voice gathered glee and pitched up. I was moved by him, less so by the universe. Incomprehensible. The blocks of our stomping grounds were mystery enough. Often too much.

***

Sam lived in an extended stay motel then. House-keeping, I said and let myself in. No one around and the bed in shambles. Strip the sheets, empty the trash, clean the bathroom. Wrote a note and stuck it to the mini-fridge with the magnet that read *Mummy...what is a Sex Pistol?*

We became friendly and occasionally more. Sam looked like Martin Sheen in *Badlands* and I had Sissy Spacek's deadpan voiceover playing in my head, so we made sense.

"I was a loser with a lot going on in my head," Sam said when I asked about San Diego. I smiled. Me too. Still was. Still am.

Sam knew everything about film. He had studied it. I mean, at matinees and drive-ins and in magazines. He worked at Four Star Video and had me over to watch movies on his VHS player. My film education: Fassbinder, Pasolini, Cassavetes, noirs, B movies, gangster pictures, midnight movies, John Waters, Richard Kern, Nick Zedd, Beth B.

He would argue movies with anyone. Once he heard a man refer to someone as the star of a docu-mentary. Sam said, "The camera is the star of the documentary." The subject then, the man said. Sam nodded, unconvinced.

Sam took me to films at the Majestic or the Frederic March Play Circle in the UW Student Union. Then we'd go see a band at O'Cayz Corral and wake up for hair of the dog at Bennett's Smut-n-Eggs for breakfast as porn played.

The end was a long ramble A numbing list of symptoms and infections. Pneumonia. Again and again. Sam was scared to be alone at night. He called me at work, hanging on the phone too long, trying to wind down and relax into sleep. When Sam didn't pick up the phone for two days, I rang the front desk. They said they couldn't go in the room. After work, I took a cab over. As it reached the stoplight across from the motel, I saw the coroner's van pull out of the driveway.

I remember the clip of Bette Davis on some talk show. "Old age ain't for sissies," she said. I think of Sam and many others. Yeah, I guess not.

***

Demarcations are form. Beginnings and endings are what grief obliterates and life tries to contain. Slippage between past and present, between one thing and another, is grief's meter. Failure is implicit. The fear of forgetting and of being forgotten, of losing still more, is the engine of grief. The hands fall off the clock. Time becomes my friends, the people I thought I was, the girl I was, the man I slip in and out of being, a hologram. They all get placed in there. How did I become the library of everyone I love?

***

Escape is vital but certainly not inward. I need to get out of here, but here is expanding and contracting: this apartment, city, night, mind, body.

I could go to the bar across the street, but my last couple visits were disappointing. The place is tiny. The wrong songs turn the atmosphere claustrophobic. I could try another bar not far from here. There will be carousing and the ranking of attraction to distract me.

I put on a coat and hat. Ready. My hand on the light switch. The terrible paralysis where every decision is a bad one, every choice an invitation to regret. Open the door and click off the light.

9

I'm half-asleep but if Dustin texts, I'm also half-awake:
a romance.

***

"You need more wickedness in your life, because you
get no rest," Dustin says.

I press him to the mattress—it's an expensive
bed—and watch his eye color change in the late afternoon light.

Dustin and I talk in a lazy way: ambitions,
movies, and places we've lived. He's lived with his
husband for eight years in two apartments and moved
once as a kid. Never lived alone.

No need for me to list all mine. I say, "I once
lived on a three-season porch for a year."

Dustin shares some childhood stories. When I
read biographies, I skip over childhood. I don't care
about your deformative years. Tell me about your escape.

Some shoplifting, cutting school, a half-assed
runaway with a straight friend he loved.

My turn: I had a cousin my same age. A big kid, much taller than me, and at holidays—Christmas usually, Easter sometimes—his mother stood us back-to-back in my grandmother's living room. My cousin was always bigger, always taller. This amused the adults. He's all-boy, my aunt said about her son. I knew what she was saying. Everyone was in on it. I pretended they didn't understand. Most are gone. The all-boy cousin too. Ten years. At his visitation I stood at his casket's side. He didn't look so big then.

My head is on Dustin's chest, his cock in my left hand, I run my right through his hair.

"A mess," he says. "I'm a mess."

"Beautiful," I say. Mouth against his jaw. I see how he will age, how the flesh will slacken, face round and droop, the smoker's lines deepen and set.

He rises to shower, doesn't invite me to join, and turns on music. A stammering rhythm and a man's high voice skim along the surface of the song. Disembodied sounds echo and submerge. I pick clothes from the floor and dress. In the kitchen I make a drink and the song shifts into another. The voice doubles and rises. *You probably thought you'd break my heart.* The shower stops. Dustin returns with damp hair, winter belly protrudes, a towel around his waist. I undo his towel, press him against the refrigerator, and we begin again.

***

Charlie insists selling off most of his possessions isn't an act of desperation, it's an act of agency. I say why not both? Desperate Agency.

He still has files of material for possible use in collages: cardboard, cutouts, pages of a dream diary, maps, papers he is attracted too, porn cocks freed from porn bodies, heads without torsos, washes of ink, tremulous lines on recipe cards, old Polaroids folded and carried in jean pockets until they creased and created something new. The layering, the placement is a religion with stations of absurdity, hallucination, deadpan jokes. Joseph Cornell wrote: "Collage = reality." Charlie calls it *the desired result*. But he hasn't made a collage in years.

An archivist might say *collections, ephemera, memorabilia, printed matter*. Charlie calls it *junk* or *My Heap*. Every time I visit, we spend an hour on show-and-tell. Sometimes the walks down memory lane are so well trod I could lip-sync along.

Charlie wears a bright multicolored mohair sweater he unearthed. "I can't believe it fits." It doesn't but he's happy. Underneath is his worn-out T-shirt emblazoned with "When I said I liked it rough I didn't mean my entire life."

He says he's living for all those who can't. The gone. I love the thought but it's not possible. You can't live for anyone else. You can't turn memories of the dead into flesh. Maybe some would contest and talk spirits, but I hear the word and picture snake handlers and river baptisms. I'll pass.

Charlie says, "Think I might move to Berlin because I don't speak the language." Silence and confusion, a true poetics, does sound appealing. He talks about there being no art, only life, which is a nifty dodge when art and life aren't working out.

I don't talk about this sense of whiplash, of being thrown out of time, and how choosing the way you'll be dismissed offers some control over your obsolescence. I say, "Are those old issues of *Outpunk*?"

***

Once Leo and I attended an art opening of terrible videos and paintings of halved natal fingerprints. He scoffed at the collages I liked. He said collage was tired. Cobbled together garbage. Yet here I am pretending to be a whole person.

***

I think of the artist who covered a huge wall with pinned record covers, concert tickets, scraps, and images of her own work linked by pieces of a pink string. A thing between a TV serial killer's obsession and a spider graph. The past mapped and tracked. She had been institutionalized as a teen and this was partially her attempt to retrace her formation. It was beautiful and ridiculous and self-obsessed and crazed. So, memory, actually.

***

A movie I remember like a dream: a man works in crucifix factory and steals the production line fuckups, mutant Christs, inverted Christs, Siamese twinned Christs crammed onto one cross. I recall nothing else about the movie. I mention it to Charlie. "Oh yeah, I vaguely remember that. The director basically disavowed the movie later." His own production line aberration.

***

Charlie has some photos of Russ Terrible.

"He was nothing special, another kid, but the moment he got in front of a camera this thing came out. Not beauty. *Glamour*. Total self-possession. Ten minutes after the shots, he was back drinking beer and mumbling dumb jokes. Someone said the reverse of Darby Crash from the Germs. He was better offstage. He was the star of the parking lot."

I remember Valentine's Day 1990. Russ was awed by the image of the earth by Voyager 1. The speck of blue like a chip in the perfect black painted wall of an S&M dungeon. A previous color and life peeping out. I put my thumb over the planet. Gone. Problem solved.

Russ headed out to cruise the buddy booths. Maybe business, maybe pleasure. I didn't judge. I would work and take my money and head to the East Village to see bands or performances. Karen Finley covered in chocolate and tinsel. Lights caught the shimmer as it shook across the stage. Like a mirror ball. Her voice rose like an evangelical preacher, shrill, piercing. Reminded me of the brim-stoner crank in the park yelling, "No hell, no dignity." But Finley's sermon was mine. I had to look away: "I wish I could relieve you of your life. I wish I could relieve you of your death."

Travel between worlds was punishing. I knew at some point the passageway would close. I knew where I wanted to be, but the other was more likely.

Russ became a dowser's wand for bad drugs and worse company. He disappeared into hotel rooms and rundown apartments with flaking walls and stained ceilings to score drugs from men named after cities—Memphis, Dallas, Branson, Houston. He tricked in a scary movie theater with stars on the ceiling that blinked in such a way they looked like they moved.

Terrible things happened. Russ vanished. No one told me to keep quiet. I knew what I thought didn't matter. I forgot because it was clear no one else remembered. To be the only one with a memory of a story others say never happened is to be crazy. I had enough problems.

***

Letting go of the past is contingent on having grasped it in the first place. I'm not sure what I have left at this point. I can't tell the difference between what I gave away, what was taken, and or what was lost. I can't distinguish between forfeiture and abandonment, reck-lessness and thoughtlessness. Someone can. There are people who know these differences, the orders of distinction in the temple of loss.

***

Try not to force things to be more than they are.
Try not to force things to be less than they are.
Try not to force things.
Try not.

***

Marking time and being marked by time. Tehching Hsieh said life is a life sentence. His art was endurance. Yearlong projects where he lived out-doors, was tied to another artist by a long rope at their waists, punched a clock every hour. He said, "This is what life is: the passage of time. It's not about how to pass the time, but about the acceptance of the time passing. People think of my work as spiritual, but it's just that I consume time. That's all."

***

I finish an article about a designer who runs eight miles every morning, eats toast for breakfast, keeps a fastidious home and appearance, and ends each night with Krug Champagne in a crystal coupe. A rigorous, regimented life. I brush crumbs off the table onto the floor and throw an apple core toward the trashcan. It misses.

***

Charlie discovered his neighbor does meditation using Tibetan singing bowls. "This should be annoying but mostly I'm relieved. I thought my tinnitus was doing something wild." Charlie sometimes identifies the pitches of his tinnitus. He tells me they're forming chords. "At night, in the quiet, they're Glenn Branca level."

***

"I miss the old Polaroids," Greer says. "No processing, no Photoshop, no fudging. You got what you got. One shot, a lottery of light and moment. Either it worked, or it didn't."

She shows me some cameras scored at estate sales and the expired film she stores in her refrigerator's crisper drawer. She tells me a trick as she selects the photos: No one looks at the camera. Place twenty photos of people not looking at the camera side by side and you have a short movie.

We talk about those artists whose daily life and experience were part of the work, all of it one project. Maybe an extinct stripe now.

Greer remembers two years when she didn't paint. "I had the shutter bug," she says. "I shook it before it ate me up."

She talks about photographic mania, the clickers who couldn't help but take endless frames leaving behind thousands of undeveloped rolls of film. The obsession to record, witness, catalogue. A way not to be human but still alive: become a camera. Brigid Berlin taped her telephone conversations, labeled, and stored thousands of cassettes in alphabetical and chronological order. She lugged her Polaroid 360 and a cumbersome cassette recorder everywhere, and said, "No picture ever mattered. It was the clicking and pulling out that I loved."

Once I helped Greer hang a show using tape, clips, pins, strings. Greer had the photos arranged chronologically but wasn't happy with it. We shuffled the photos like a deck of cards and hung them that way. Accidents. A critic reviewed it later and talked about ephemera and transience and fragility. Greer was broke and thought it looked cool.

***

Charlie shows me his autograph collection and we talk about our favorite celebrity deaths. I was obsessed by Jayne Mansfield's as a kid. Crash-scene photos showed her wig tangled in the car's windshield and those fueled the rumors that she'd been decapitated, which wasn't true. But that story fit in nicely beside the urban legends of my childhood, like "Mama Cass" Elliot choking to death on a sandwich (it was a heart attack) or Rod Stewart getting his stomach pumped of semen after servicing a group of sailors (sadly, untrue). But the one I love for its sheer camp value is Jean Cocteau dying from a heart attack upon hearing the news of Edith Piaf's death the day before. A royal exit.

***

Greer's favorite TV interview was when Barbara Walters asked Katharine Hepburn if she owned a skirt and Hepburn replied, "I'll wear it to your funeral."

Greer scrawls the reply on a piece of paper with a quick sketch while working on a painting. Her asides and takeaways, as she dismissively calls them, are my secret favorites. She treats them like handouts or flyers. Here, she says, and gives me Red Riding Dyke chatting up the butch wolf. "My, what big hands you have." She signs them all Charlie Best or Tilden Smith (Jean Rhys's married name). Her Miss Nomer cartoon panels are magneted to my fridge, holding up my work schedule. Everything marked in pencil.

***

Greer sketches prop planes while listening to a playlist of Buddy Holly, Patsy Cline, and Otis Redding tunes.

She made a studio visit to a young woman recently out of art school who asked for advice. Greer said, "To have freedom and make work and live for experience means damage. You'll get knocked around, punished, ignored, worse. But it's worth it."

"How'd she take that?" I say.

"She asked if I knew any gallerists to represent her."

***

Pleasant drunk man leaving the Dilly Dally says, "Stay you, man."

Are there other options? I'd like to hear them before I make the lazy choice.

10

Soundtrack: Julie London, French pop, car alarms. Dustin and I had plans, but he canceled an hour ago, so I'm getting cocktails alone. I will probably drink until I forget dinner and myself, sliding into the sweet spot where I disappear. My booth has a small tea candle that flickers in the cold air each time the door opens. The sky has changed from gray to charcoal, quick streamers of cloud to heavy cover. Impermanence is good.

An older man sits at the bar. Might be my age. Might be younger. Heavy drinker. He looks like half my customers at the Dilly Dally. He's on his third drink since I arrived. Doesn't strike me as sad or lonely. None of the sentimentality of one drinker looking at another. I'm not drunk enough yet.

Rastafarians believe the body is a temple. They don't drink alcohol because they believe fermented foods turn the body into a cemetery. Mine is probably a mausoleum in low-lying flood plains where the water can't free the gardens of the dead.

Empty glass and a decision must be made. Another or go somewhere else or join the drunk at the bar and accept fate.

***

Dustin texts. His husband went through his phone and saw our texts and flipped out.

—Don't you have an open marriage?

—We do but we're supposed to tell each other everything and I haven't about you.

A supercut of cock pics and the explicit texts—my beard, your balls, my face, your ass. Dumb porn language from a dumb porn person. My sweat smells metallic.

—I'm fucking torn up. I'm sorry this happened. I'm going to work. Going to talk with him more when I get home.

My mind reads off a Teleprompter. What I could say I mean but the words are used up, beyond secondhand. I am a cliché. An older man having a non-affair with a younger man. A lonely man in a lousy room saying tired words.

***

I tell Charlie I never thought I'd get to be an adulteress.

"We have come so far as a people," he says.

***

Dustin sends a cock pic from the bathroom of the hotel.

—I'm hard thinking of you.

I'm hardly awake.

He says he wants to see me after work. I avoid the porno spiel and we make a plan.

I run water for a shower and stand before the mirror staring at the gray bristling in my beard. I step into the shower and am taken aback for a moment, not by the temperature or the strength but by the fact of the water. This is the problem lately: life is not real.

I soap my armpits and stare at my limp cock: *I'm hard*.

***

Dustin cancels hanging out. Clandestine goes boom.

— I can't see you or contact you for a while. I don't know when. I'm sorry, I feel awful about everything.

***

As soon as I walk up the steps and pull the door open, I know I've made a mistake. The bar is busy. Two spots, one wedged between an animated man with a booming fake-sounding laugh and another at the end of the bar's horseshoe by the corridor to the women's bathroom. I claim the toilet-adjacent, drape my coat over the barstool, climb onto it clumsily. The man next to me nods and returns to watching the muted TV. A generic rock song from a decade ago with a plodding rhythm and hoarse vocals plays. I order, pull out my phone, and scroll texts I haven't answered. Earlier conversations hanging in suspension. I survey predictable action until my drink appears.

Dustin and his husband walk in. My body stiffens. His husband notices me, and his look turns hard. Voices in the room rise at the game on TV. He speaks to Dustin, who doesn't look over, but pivots and turns his back toward me. They leave.

I finish my drink in one slug. The bartender gives me a crooked smile. He points at my empty glass, and I mouth yes.

***

I check my phone periodically hoping for a text from Dustin, an acknowledgment he saw me last night and felt strange and awkward and helpless. What I want is to still exist.

***

Sobered up, unable to slow enough to sleep though I am leaden.

I listen to a cover of "It's All Over Baby Blue," by Marianne Faithfull. Last year, I was in the ER with a kidney stone. The morphine kicked in and I hummed one of her songs.

Leo once told me "Bob Dylan is god."

I said, "That makes sense because I don't like his followers either."

"You are a disrespecter," he said again and again. Not *disrespectful*. *Disrespecter*, like the name of a garage band, overlooked and forgotten, or perhaps celebrated by a cultish following and insular critics.

I loved Dylan but he was *spiritual* for Leo. He spoke of many places—the Southwest, northern Canada, Ireland—and artists, poets, and thinkers as spiritual. He saw himself on a path to enlightenment, a whole system of thinking—maybe even belief—I rejected. His transformation was undetectable in anything other than words of intention. He wanted change and he strove to capture and quantify it, to make it happen, whereas I have mostly witnessed change happen on its own. The deep shifts in people's lives are unstoppable.

Nothingness. "You like that word—nothing—don't you?" Leo said one night. "You say it all the time."

The void as a constant, a worry stone, a tic. I wouldn't know how to reach for the transcendental. I only wanted to sit and smoke and talk about movies and bands.

Leo asked how I could believe in nothing. How could I not? Nothingness is enormous and impossible. All that endless silence, much bigger than god. I said if there were a god it would be a force that didn't answer to the word god, was not in any way anthropomorphic, most definitely was not involved in human matters, and was beyond our comprehension and even love as we understood it. The idea a force that large and abstract would love me as an individual or feel my love was absurd. And even if that force existed, I still believed my consciousness would be snuffed by my death and "I" would no longer exist.

Leo was quiet, and I thought, I should start telling people I believe in god and explain it that way.

The playlist has gotten maudlin, so I switch to Alice Coltrane, then Sun Ra.

Dear Humans, my report is complete. Thank you for your hospitality and for showing me your ways. I am heading home. Be well.

***

The end didn't feel like an end so that's where I ended it.

In Chicago, my boyfriend and I were in the car at the end of a long evening during which I had gotten drunk and quiet at a party. The party had been a smattering of his friends and important people who could be useful. I was tired of the maneuvering and the alignments and the allegiances. I was tired of scrambling all the time. I was tired of him.

He asked me why I had been quiet, and I said because I didn't trust anyone there, but added, "I trust you. I'm just tired. Long week."

The weeks had all turned long, and I didn't trust him. I matched his distance with my own. I didn't need, even when hurt, to lash out with some bitchy remark. I was biding time. What I was waiting for was unknown. I watched traffic. Soon I would be asleep or at least in bed. I reached over and held his hand.

***

The fag end of the relationship, read the sentence. British. Fag meaning cigarette. I once explained to someone that the word faggot came from the bundles of sticks Christians used to burn homosexuals, heretics, and witches. I stopped hating the men who called me faggot on the street and began to hate the bystanders, the ones around who did nothing, who laughed or frowned or averted their eyes. The fire was strong that year. I hadn't yet found a way to live in the world. I hadn't yet discovered heroin.

***

How many times: packed, waiting to leave, thought I'd missed something. A last-minute list of possible objects. Nothing. I had what I had.

***

"The first time I heard this song was in Paris."

The man has been talking for a while. His spiel is crafted for an audience of young provincials who confuse talk of money with money. For this strain of talker, it is never enough to mention a night out without saying the anecdotal bar was in Barcelona. He talks about the English seaside and artists he knows in Berlin. An eager young guy listens closely, gaining brightness. This would be the one the man snags for this story. The reward for his worldliness is a kid who wants out any way possible. But you never get to fuck the story.

The kid wears rumpled clothes and has a knapsack tucked at his feet. He nurses a drink and sways to the music. His face catches the light and looks like it could cut any surface.

A strange protectiveness. I want to warn him. What would I say? That he's young and has his whole life ahead of him? He doesn't. Only a newborn has his whole life ahead of him, and even then, he is burdened by his mother's body, his father's genes, his region, his class. The more I think of it, the more the baby's life shrinks. As they clear his throat and judge his color and alertness, his future is set.

I could tell the kid something useful. Charge more, carry a blade, and if things turn ugly, say you were robbed not raped. The kid looks at me. I must have been staring. His diamond face is blank or annoyed or blankly annoyed. He will be dried out like a wishbone and broken for fun. I rattle my drink's ice, take one last sip, and leave.

Outside momentum carries me. My pulse is quick. Wet, heavy snow is falling. The sidewalks are thick, and I struggle. The wind has picked up and I bear down, headlong into the gusts. I don't stop walking until I reach my building.

The lock won't budge, and I fear it has been changed, something vile is happening, a repeat of old bad times but diced up and rearranged into a new horror. It succumbs to the key on the fifth try. I stagger up the stairs, stopping at the landing as my knees give, I brace my arm on the loose banister and some plaster crumbles. It dusts my wet boots. I let myself in, half expecting someone or something to be there, waiting.

11

Black dog on the bed. Owl on the windowsill. I'm sure it's nothing.

Tonight is going to be one of those days. My mind burned through a sleeping pill like it was a Tic Tac. I'm stranded here on my bed like a life raft. It's late and all I do is place one foul thought next to another. Awake, thinking and thinking, like editing the same paragraph over and over. I guess dawn is stet, but that's a long night.

***

Please keep all hands, feet, arms, and legs inside the ride at all times. Let's pretend context still means something. And my vulnerability is my philosophy in action. Or at least vibration. Life math: the number of things I don't understand, the number of things I've accepted, the number of things I've denied, the number of things I've failed.

***

Don't take life advice from anyone who is a parent—they're under contract to believe in a future. The mirages created by childhood indoctrination: there are lessons to be learned in everything, all loose ends neatly tied, a place where everything belongs.

I read about a twenty-seven-year-old anti-natalist who sued his parents for creating him without his consent. I don't believe in an afterlife, but I'll entertain the thought of a process server in heaven.

A lot of what I get upset about is the future and in practical terms I have no biological investment in one. Sometimes when I watch the news, I remind myself I haven't loved this country since I was a fourteen-year-old pariah in the 1980s and its citizens wanted me dead. Good luck with your society, I wrote on a T-shirt then. The kid still makes me smile.

I used to say there are not good people, only good actions. I no longer believe that. There are not good people or good actions. There are actions whose harms are not yet known. Helpers are mostly hurters with delusions of goodness and humility. Acts of kindness are only that—acts.

I try to think what I know without any doubt. This: to have the life force battered out of you, the will to live sapped, the connections severed until the only path is retreat, the only pulse survival, then to be told you aren't alive enough, you are negative, an abyss by the batterers, sappers, and severers is to be driven mad. Turn the knife outward, I say.

***

Cathartic sounds positively academic for what I require. How did this happen? A little at a time? All at once? Does it matter? This is the way it is. How it was arrived at won't change the fact.

***

I replay things to wear them down, take the edges off, and make them smaller, handheld.

Two-timing on all my thoughts today. The line between resilience and delusion is especially blurry. Thoughts pile up, overlap, circle back to something old and painful and pair it to something fresh and bright. There, my mind says, those go together. Matchy-matchy. Separated by twenty years but the same because tonight's lesson is nothing has changed. Not only have I not amounted to anything, I never have been anything.

Comforting in a way. I will follow the natural trajectory of my nothingness. As close to momentum as I will get.

You can be fucked now, or you can be fucked hard later. I berate myself like a dumb dom from central casting.

***

Something moves alongside the day: a shadow. A memory. Fear not formulated into thought. Flimsy life cruising along low to the ground.

It's not as bad as it was before. Last year I was electric and raised, like the air before a storm. Tension kept me up at night until the fog came. Flatness, an emptying, took over.

Thoughts like *you have wasted your entire life* had the authority of fact and offer a horrible relief. I pretended my life was happening to someone else. Someone I disliked a lot.

The air was close. The sheets were filthy. I drank from dirty glasses. I ate tuna from the can with a snaggle-tined fork. I moved from bed to bathroom with great effort. I smelled bad but couldn't bring myself to shower or even whore-bathe at the sink. The world was only marginalia.

What I experienced was not shared by those around me. Nothing new. I'd rarely been on the same plane as others. Too sensitive, people had said. I perceived my dreams as memories, as events I believed had happened. My waking life was a lucid dream, and my dreams were actual. I knew it wasn't right even though it was real.

The winnowed sensation. I was paring down to a single thought. Cutting through the numbness was the determination I had run my course. I saw it clearly: the way a space might open perfectly sized to me, and I didn't even have to move toward it. Its gravitational force pulled me. Neat, really.

On the bridge before dawn, the barrier was six feet high. I stood on my toes and took the measure of my self–destruction.

***

Bedlamite. Noun. Archaic. British English. A lunatic; insane person.

Bedlamite sodomite: Crazy fucker.

If you aren't the crazy fucker in someone else's story, what sort of life are you living?

***

The French chanteuse said, "I am happy when I sing a sad song and sad when I sing a happy song. When you sing a song that is up, where can you go but down? But if you sing a song that is down, where can you go but up?" Once asked why his songs were so sad, the folk singer said, "Oh, they're not all so sad. Some of them are just hopeless. The other ones are sad."

***

I go to a strenuously life-affirming movie with Avery. It's a quiet, mostly middle-aged white crowd smattered with gay men who came for the fiercesome diva turn of the aging leading lady and perhaps for the vealcake who struts through the film and cries drunkenly on his best buddy's shoulder in the cathartic sensitive-male scene. The audience murmurs as they exit the theater and check their phones. I pick it apart afterward and Avery says, "What did you expect?" Finding something vapid and pointing it out is not an empty gesture. It's a gesture at emptiness.

***

Without premeditation, out of laziness, indecision, and dread of the weekend grocery store, I have eaten two slices of toast, some pretzel sticks, a handful of popcorn, and a couple jellybeans: *A Charlie Brown Thanksgiving*. I change from pajamas to pants and a shirt, then get back into bed fully dressed. Much better under a mound of blankets with endless movies queued up in an empty apartment. Thankful.

***

I watch a show about the Yellowstone supervolcano that will kill us all. Very relaxing. I have channeled my terror about impending civil war into buying bootleg T-shirts of No Wave bands and lifting weights with the goal of looking like a buff garden gnome. My fear of commitment keeps me from embracing the apocalypse.

***

Trying to knock things off my to-do list, but already I'm losing ground within one phone call: "Before we delete the personal information as requested, can you tell us a little bit about yourself?"

***

Favorite words at the Dilly Dally: *facts* and *truth*. People invoke them as indisputable vantages. Breast-beating lunacy. I want to say define your terms. By facts do you mean dates and sequences and exact words spoken? From my experience, people are bad at remembering. When we retell a story, it's usually only the memory of the last time we told the same story. Each telling floats farther away from its source material. Well, there in my choice of words—source material—you see part of the problem. I don't believe there is any such thing as non-fiction. The footage is always edited. Angle, agenda, aesthetics. My distrust stems from years when what I experienced was so radically rewritten by others, I ceased trusting anyone. Even myself.

For years after I left my mother's house, I would have strobe-like spells where I saw the scene from outside like watching a film with me as a character. After, I returned to the interior of the character, but the split—the knowledge of the character, the puppetry involved in the practiced hand of reality—remained. Often, it was seamless, and the appearance of a cohesive person was intact. Other times, something revealed itself, the foreignness living within, and the way minutes and hours did not pass in anything like standard time.

I say nothing. I don't probe their truths or facts. I do side work.

***

Is it a bad sign when you can't imagine using drugs because they seem too life-affirming? I sometimes still dream of being a gentleman junkie, a dandy in a cravat with a long cigarette ash. A horrible thought: Nothing will ever hold me as well as heroin did. Everything and everyone will be pale flickers I project longing on. Most of my heroin years were awful, but for a brief time the high was the best sensation I had ever had. And I can never have it again.

***

I am a fatalist who cannot accept his fate. My horoscope says, "You will find interacting with others is a source of great inspiration now." Inspiration is an elastic term.

***

"*Squib load*: a firearm malfunction in which a fired projectile does not have enough force behind it to exit the barrel, and thus becomes stuck. This type of malfunction can be extremely dangerous, as failing to notice that the projectile has become stuck in the barrel may result in another round being fired directly into the obstructed barrel, resulting in a catastrophic failure of the weapon's structural integrity."

Relatable.

***

"Only god can judge me," I say.

"You don't believe in god," Charlie says.

"Exactly."

When I was young and believed, I thought god heard and organized, numbered, and rated the thoughts of all people. The impossible noise. Within the fantasy of an all-knowing, all-hearing god, the cacophony would turn into an indecipherable hum, then the sound of ringing. Humanity as tinnitus.

***

"Knowing when to leave is the most important thing" is good advice, but it's taken on a different tone, a larger meaning. Leave now?

Avery speaks about making a commitment to life. I can, of course, and I do. I'm here, aren't I? But we're all in an open relationship with death.

Greer says the words depression and anxiety have been decanted of meaning, turned into possessions: My Depression, My Anxiety. A badge. Diagnosis as astrology.

Take something for the pain. Define something. Define pain.

Get over yourself said to someone who has no idea who they are.

If you see only the contradictions and hypocrisies surrounding us you risk morality, and if you see only the contradictions and hypocrisies in yourself you risk insensibility. Someone will tell you the balance is to see both and find some acceptance in the knowledge. I am not that person.

***

I watched part of a British home show and the phrase "Smarten up your flat with a coat of paint" stuck. Now

I have six little test stripes on my wall and no will to wise up.

***

Who needs horror movies? All you have to do is live long enough. The shift over time from the question of *if* we know ourselves to *how* we know ourselves is the true terror. My greatest fear? The hierarchy of fear. Having one thing I fear most means I'm not paying attention. I'm negligent to the world.

***

It is what it is, as some would say. And while I agree with them—accepting what is before me for its true nature—I'd also remove myself from their presence as soon as possible. It's important to keep a sense of possibility, even if it's a delusion. Those who envision and promote themselves as realists are the most dangerous fabulists.

***

I feel like I slept through an earthquake but there was no earthquake, and I didn't sleep.

My mind has slowed from a movie to a slideshow, the sound of the carousels, the click, the light and black and light again. Some images still stun.

I have hardly left a four-block radius. My life is a prism of lines—work, store, post office, bank—the uncomplicated web of an old spider who can no longer pull a path from its body. The list of things to avoid grows and grows. Movement in the world gets smaller. If I stay in this room, if I don't leave, if I don't speak to anyone, the spell will remain unbroken. I will maintain the illusion of an accord between thoughts and actions. Mostly because I'm not taking any actions.

Hours have slacked, as if there is a little carbon monoxide leak. The day is squandered, and the night lies out before me, impossible. I'm frozen, unable to move forward, unable to take hold of anything because then I'll be vulnerable to losing it.

I lie down and admire the abandoned test patches of paint along the wall. The multicolored starts and stops are clumpy in spots like a topographical map. I haven't been able to settle on a color. Another cigarette. All my opinions turn to ash and start over.

***

I look at my shelves: these books, these things, I know, only offer a false sense of security, the mistaken identity of having for being. I'm a have-not reverse slumming for this year and maybe another. Eventually these books and boxes will have to go. They will stand in the way of my project, which isn't forgetting or remembering but making. I have another book to make, another day. These things are vestiges of different times and people who aren't around. I'm here and they aren't. It's as simple and as complicated as that.

12

I remember a photo of a typed card from the New York Public Library information desk. It read: What is the life expectancy of the abandoned woman? I'm neither but I would like an estimate, please.

***

Expectant, I look at my phone, then across the street at a passerby heading to the corner store, hoping for Dustin. I want the intervals between glances at my phone and the street to grow until I don't look.

***

I found out my younger, much taller crush's nickname for me is Father Figurine. I accept that.

"Daddy, I love your mustache."

I don't tell him the way it curls down reminds me of Jeanne Moreau's downturned mouth. I feel like a gorgeous French woman.

***

Things not to say on apps:

I'm not your daddy, I'm just old.

I'm the age where existential moments of "What am I doing with my life?" can only be answered with (whispered) "Heading toward death."

In middle-age, a fourgy sounds like a lot of work.

The only thing I am capable of nurturing are grudges.

I'm not your future, I'm your night.

***

Catering, I explain poor life decisions to someone who is the age I was when I made them and realize I can't simply blame mine on being young. And now know that when I was in my twenties the forty-somethings I knew showed incredible restraint by not telling me about the aging process. I don't impart any life lessons. I present myself as Exhibit A.

***

My only question today: Do you dislike linear time because you fear aging?

As I've gotten older, people have said I've gotten kinder. It's not kindness, it's indifference.

On her 1970 live album *Black Gold*, Nina Simone introduces "Who Knows Where The Time Goes" by saying, "Time is a dictator as we know it. Where does it go? What does it do? Most of all, is it alive?"

Avery gave me a moisturizer called Midnight Recovery Concentrate. I apply it at noon so it can ramp up to its magical bewitching hour.

***

Life distinctions:
Childhood: spanked and put to bed with no supper.
Adulthood: pay for the privilege and the privation.

***

On a date, a man told me he was enigmatic. Imagine sitting across from another human being and saying such a thing. I fucked him for his hubris. I wore him out. No mystery sweats that much.

***

Mating repartee:

Him: Just a thought.

Me: Barely.

***

Avery quotes *Camille*, a play by Charles Ludlam: "Have you no heart, Marguerite?" He takes the role of Marguerite: "I'm travelling light!"

***

"My friendships are my romantic life," Charlie says.

"That's another way to be heartbroken," I say.

"I love you like a brother."

"In a French movie way?"

Charlie talks about an old boyfriend. "He treated my love as a burden, so I stopped burdening him. You know me, I'm not very free about feelings but I was a goddamn ballad compared to him."

"I've dated a few of those. Instrumentals. They're usually the guys who proudly say that they don't cry, which means they're hitters."

***

Two drinks in, Charlie and I have wandered off road conversationally and are discussing shame. As a teen he was told by a nun that because he was an obvious homosexual he would burn in hell for eternity. "I figured, well, it doesn't matter what I do then, so I'll do whatever I please. And in the end Sister Mary Dorothy had a catastrophic stroke and lived for two years unable to move or talk. So, there was a happy ending."

Charlie calls anyone he considers a judger Mary Dorothy.

His devout mother asked him, "What will you say when Jesus returns?"

"When will this guy learn?"

I tell Charlie I don't remember the Scripture thrown at me as a kid. Genesis, Leviticus, Romans, Kings? More? Why would I recall such poorly writ-ten trash. The Bible isn't even mediocre literature. Shoddy magical realism at best. Closer to an LSD trip book by a lesser Warhol superstar.

Hell ended belief for me at thirteen. Eternal damnation and hellfire? How silly. Once I began pulling on the thread faith unraveled. You believe you sit in a box with chicken wire between you and a man in a dress and he gives you some spells to say and you are forgiven by an imaginary dad, but I will live in a lake of fire (I do not understand how that works) for eternity (please define) for existing? And I am meant to consider you as an adult human and argue this with you?

"What's the point in suffering if there isn't love too?" Charlie says.

"Some people are in love with their suffering. I mean, they learn to love it because they understand nothing else is coming."

"Well damn, I need another drink. You?"

"A double."

***

Greer says she deserves a medal for being a lesbian who has never had a live-in girlfriend. "It's my true achievement. Do you have any idea the social pressure to pair off and shack up? I've spent decades taking shit for not wanting to play house. Women think there's something wrong with you even as they serial monogamize into the sun. Or hit bed death in seven years and stay in a chaste hand-holding sisterly life eating their feelings and resenting everyone. Congratulations, you gave the patriarchy a makeover."

***

The day in, day out, year after year of domestic life and the idea of another person as your half, as the listener and speaker, the comforter and agitator, the one who knows more of you than you could bear, does occasionally appeal to me. Sometimes making food, shaving, unloading groceries, I wish someone were in my way. Wanting this, seeking this, and living this are three separate things. Three lives maybe.

***

"Your wife is a lucky man" were the last words Avery texted to his married man. "I was the homo-sexual Hamburger Helper to spice up his marriage," Avery says. A little fucking, a little sucking, a late-night rim job in a public parking structure."

Greer says, "I've been down that road before. Both sides of that road. Straight girls are the worst, of course, but I also had a former girlfriend—a staunchly righteous lesbian separatist of the early '90s Madison, Wisconsin variety—who ended up with a man. Her rich family cut off her and within a month she cartwheeled onto a dick. Ah, sisterhood."

***

A coworker talks about marriage. I hardly muster ambivalence. I say there were too many years of it being held as something sacred and special and therefore withheld so I wrote it off. He clearly sees me as a bitter old queen (guilty on all three counts) spouting some outdated nonsense. Just you wait, I want to say, playing exactly to type.

***

Overheard: "He was talking about living life to the fullest and all I could think about was how fat he'd gotten."

***

The headline: "Should I tell my fiancée that I'm bisexual and had sex with her dad?"

No, but text me.

***

In a boutique hotel with Hugh in the shower. I'm under the crisp white sheet and voices from down the hall and on the street drift in and out. This is like the psych ward.

"Is that guy checking out you or me?" Avery says.

"There's a mirror behind us."

"Anyway, with this guy I also think I'm pretending or something."

"Why not? I mean slip in and out of the mask. It's all part of the way we find our desires. As gay men we're always performing. What's bad about that? We're show people."

"How did you know there were masks involved?"

***

My young friend texts: "The top I had a crush on, who would sleep over, cuddle, have meals with me, and told me how much he loves hanging with me for the last two months, just dropped he's in a long-distance relationship by inviting me to a threesome with them."

***

This bar's motto should be: *Swing your dick and hit a loser.*

The man wears a T-shirt for the Wreck Room, Milwaukee's first cowboy/leather/Levi's bar, which opened in July 1972. He says he's Midwest sober: beer only. An alcoholic with control issues—how original. His banter comes down to: shame is in the eye of the scolder, we're all members of the Mutual Degradation Society, and most moral codes are simply vanity. On the TV an old movie plays without sound. Subtitles. A man with a pencil-thin mustache says, "They went hell for leather. They wanted to be the best and they wanted to be wild."

This night has become a dunk tank without water. I excuse myself to the bathroom. A manifesto on the stall wall: "Fags, learn how to suck Cock good. The best hobby on Earth for Fags to do with others. It's free. Requires only the equipment you are born with, needs no prep or clean up, last hours or minutes, releases chemicals in your body that reduce stress. Can be done anywhere. And builds relationships. Suck more Cock!"

We aren't even flesh, we're utensils. But I like feeling useful.

He's gone when I return, and I watch the parade of everyone who isn't going to get what they want. Astral diva voices pierce the bar with songs of lost love, love gone wrong, love everlasting. I take a seat by the exit, ready to make my move.

***

This guy looks like trouble, by which I mean "Hello."

The fantasy is quiet desperation, with the emphasis on *quiet*. No problem. Some talk but they have nothing much to say. The expanse of silence is the true language, with music and glasses clinking and water running. Words have no place unless they are sung on the jukebox.

Pool balls align and scatter. I watch his knuckles work the stick and move around between good and bad light, so he understands I'm ugly but I'm confidant. Two fingers of bourbon bring some courage. Close to him, I place my hand on his. My hand is a thin scribble on a thick fact.

He grins, a shadow on the right where some teeth are missing shows. That's better. Broken beauties and crazies are the best fucks.

We finish the game and walk to my apartment. He doesn't care my place is a dump. Him inside the door. Him on me. Don't bother with music or another drink. Atmosphere is for faggots. Push him against the wall. He grunts. His submission is a game. Twice my size but lets me push him around a little bit before he grabs my throat, kicks my legs apart, and forces me to my knees.

We roughhouse for an hour, winding up and down. I put his hand on my throat, and he squeezes and relaxes his grip.

"Keep going," I say.

After he leaves, I get back in bed, lying my head next to the damp spot and freckles of red. My arms and legs pulse and a bite mark on my wrist glistens between blinks that grow longer until I fade.

13

The odometer in my head turns over. A friend in New York who I hear from twice a year sends a flurry of messages, then vanishes. I picture his cramped apartment. Esoteric ephemera and memorabilia, a constellation of minor stars and forgotten faces on the edge of memory staring down. Long-ago shared interests: hard drugs, cheap beers, strange fucks. Dissolute living has given way to living, or something best left to the imagination.

***

My days are a blur of Dilly Dally shifts where regulars play dice games for happy hour deals. The job is like a gas station bathroom. I'm there because I have to be, and I made poor choices leading up to it. The bar flies are my Sunday matinee crowd and I give them to the best of my limited acting abilities what they want.

Dream-dreaming love-loving songs fill the room, punch the air with determined little fists of notes, ripple out into palsied vibrato signifying vulnerability. I play favorites. They are frozen, a hermetic loop of pain and transcendence, longing and movement. A song I haven't heard in a while comes on. I don't like what this one means. I have aged and it hasn't. It reminds me of Leo. One of his spirituals. It wasn't a song of his and it wasn't from our time together, but it has expanded to take his world in and replaced the sounds of then.

***

I know working class self-educated people should avoid people who measure time by semesters or quarterly reports. Sometimes I forget because I need to eat or fuck.

***

During my afternoon shift at the Dilly Dally, I listen to scraps of conversation and hear someone—a movie star, a pop singer, someone the word icon or diva is attached to—described as ageless. When it's said someone's ageless, I assume it means they're dead.

***

Busy work. I make my wish list, shit list, chore list, stud file. Then the friend count of who cares. Then why. That undoes some of the concerned. Mottos: Do no harm but take no shit. Avoid anthems, awards, flags, nations, prayers, slogans, teams. I rewrite my app bio: I can take a dick. I can take a joke. I can take a dick joke. I can take a joke dick.

***

Not working Sunday brunch shift so Arthur Russell is my church/tea dance/lunar landing. I will dance badly—let's call it movement—around my apartment in tatty clothes and avoid my phone for as long as possible. Maybe even reward myself with a cigarette.

***

My old peacoat with blown-out pockets has aged a decade in the last year. I'm online coveting a puffer that looks either like the night sky or oil in a puddle. Fortunately, this mistake is beyond my budget.

***

Catering a queer winter wedding and everyone talks about the beauty of the queer winter wedding, how unique it is, not like a queer summer wedding. A woman tells another woman, "It's funny because there are no wedding ceremonies in the Bible for centuries straight couples have adapted the oaths of Ruth and Naomi or David and Jonathan. Or used Shakespeare's Sonnet 18's shall I compare thee to a summer's day, which is explicitly written to a young man."

I almost prefer the hyper-straight weddings to this. Almost.

***

Winterlude: My tradition of checking flights to New Orleans and Los Angeles has begun. I rebuffed an invite to a bar night called Beards of Paradise so I'm home wearing a Snoopy cap bundled under covers trying to get the best deal for my imaginary trip.

I rouse for a cigarette. Holiday chilli pepper lights are strung in the garden. Cheap green plastic lawn chairs stake the piled snow. What looks like a headless snake, or a monster umbilical cord made by Eva Hesse sits by the trashcans. Then the syringe glints bright. I guess the front security door isn't latching and the junkies are coming through to the backyard for some privacy, or the guy on the first floor is at it again. Sloppy.

If there's a war on Christmas, where do I enlist?

***

A good night to make dinner, leave the dishes, and walk around the block alone in the cold whispering "Fuck it all." The temperature is twenty-seven degrees, but it feels like sixteen with eleven mile an hour winds from the northwest, according to the weather app on the phone. That is why the phone was left on the counter. Who needs a companion like that?

The spiral: stop fucking around, get real, move. Or: heavier blanket, better novels, stronger light.

***

Briefly joined a tobogganless luge event while taking the trash out at work. Weirdly exhilarated, possibly concussed. Hot date with an Epsom bath later.

***

Catering a reunion. There's a deadness to these events. Everything is recorded by some means, and no one is natural or loose. The attendees angle for the best light.

Maybe this is part of why going out in public is fraught—performance anxiety. The only time I could imagine a reunion being joyous is if it involved buried loot from a bank heist.

I walk around humming "Pirate Jenny." Don't mind me. In back the servers compare which brand of frozen peas we use to ice our knees. I'm old school and just plain old: Birds Eye.

***

Mark E Smith of the Fall said, "I used to be psychic, but I drank my way out of it," which is the opposite of the people who believe they drink themselves into insights and second sights. They ring the bar this afternoon.

A man tells a bobsled slick tale of how he broke his neck and was confined to a halo brace for six months, and later underwent a C1-C2 fusion. Glasses raised, man. A survivor.

I crave contrarians and curmudgeons. The anti-intellectualism I love requires scorn for the worlds of school and work and loves being omnivorously, idiosyncratically well-read with a battered public library card tucked in your wallet.

A self-reminder: Sir/Madam, it's four in the afternoon in Riverwest in Milwaukee, Wisconsin. Read the room, block, neighborhood, city, county, state, country. This is not your home.

***

A customer at the Dilly Dally gives advice to a new arrival from the west coast. "If you enter a mid-western home and see a folksy wood sign that reads *I'll pour you a glass of get over it and here's a straw to suck it up,* run like your life depends on it—it does."

They end up swapping stories of childhood humiliation and shame. Tales with honed laugh lines. I was always ashamed but not sufficiently ashamed for my mother's taste.

The woman who ran the nursery school I attended called my mother concerned because I played the Mother in games of house. I liked being female and I liked being the star of the show.

My mother came to the school and observed me from behind a two-way mirror. Afterward she cried and yelled in the car. What is wrong with you? The next day I didn't play.

It was the beginning of a recurring dream. I was in bed immobile with the covers pulled up to my chin I couldn't move anything except my eyes. The bed was under a high rectangular window and a man and a woman stood side by side either outside or inside the window laughing at me. I lay in bed paralyzed. Only my eyes moved, and the man and woman laughed until I closed them and woke.

I utter not a word of it. Not a shareable anecdote. "Another round?"

***

At a certain age it isn't flouting conventional respectability, it's your life. There's no resolution between the individual and society. All you have is your meager person, your little agency, mostly oppressed but still beating if you desire. The only choice is between living in your own struggle or in the ones other people inflict.

All of this is to say my tips were dismal today and I heard the stock Wisconsin phrases "You can't win for losing" and "They get you coming, and they get you going" repeatedly.

***

People with patchy histories are my people. At forty, I lost my job, apartment, most of my possessions. Starting over felt impossible. So, I didn't. I let the drift take me. It's not refusal to assimilate if they'd never have you anyway.

***

Pack up, pawn off, save tips, split town, but I've run out of places to go. It's too expensive. I can't pass a credit check. I can't do the paperwork. I have to know someone, have some connection—no matter how fritzed—who can vouch for me or cut a deal. A sublet on a place in limbo after developers went bankrupt. An artist studio with a kitchen and bathroom down the hall that isn't zoned for living but that's solved by a futon couch and not getting too homey.

***

A regular wonders, "How much of the game do you have to play, and how much can you play against the game?" It isn't a game for me.

***

Things they say too far into the night to turn back:

"My father was monster when I was a child. Running away from home was my only way out. Leaving behind my little sister still haunts me."

"Of course, he never loved me. He only loved himself."

"What's the point of it, you know?"

The *you-knows* grow more emphatic. Gestures more pointed.

Last call. Last call for alcohol.

***

Charlie gives me an early birthday gift. An old album we both love reissued on vinyl. Listening, I find one song has lyrics which were imprinted on my brain as a private motto since I was fifteen: There are no answers / only reasons to be strong.

***

Ten degrees. Cigarette smoke in cold air is my meditation.

Walking home from work last night was like skating and the city looked like a breathing jewel. Today it's back to windblown tundra and snow trudgery.

I'm not going to take it for granted when the snow finally melts and I can take long, pointless walks again.

One advantage to the frigid weather is the muggings of the summer—a mix of desperate junkies and teen gang initiations—have gone into hibernation. Although not all. Last winter after I went to Circle A for Charlie's monthly DJ stint I was chased by a young man. "Can I ask you a question?" he yelled down the block. My stylish shoes had little tread and as usual the lazy drunkards of the neighborhood had neglected shoveling so a layer of packed down snow and ice covered the sidewalks. I moved in place like a cartoon. He was closer, then he fell. I got ahead. He called me a faggot and a bitch. A faggotbitch. I made it to Locust Street and ran across in a brief gap of hurtling traffic. Turning back, I saw my pursuer round the corner and I dodged down an alley, fiddled with the back-door lock of my building. Inside my apartment I was frantic and furious. Before long adrenaline leeched away. Sapped, I went to bed. I didn't dream of him.

***

I wander past a house with a lit-up ornamental cross in the yard. Wrong part of the story.

I stopped marking the holidays long ago. The secular celebrations are an absurd pantomime. I order Chinese food, watch movies, and nap until it's over and Christmas trees line the curbs.

I dodder along snowy ice-slicked paths and curse. One of my Dilly Dally duties is shoveling. A rhythm of misery and tendonitis. My wrist and forearm are wrapped under my sweatshirt's sleeve. Zigzag past some desperate construction sites of emergency street and sewage repairs. Segments of large pipes rest in a vacant slushy lot looking like a derelict playground for hard-up kids.

Supposedly a blizzard is bearing down. The news reports are alarmed and glib with scenarios of shutdowns, accidents, and downed power lines. People have rushed the grocery stores to stock up. I hear the between-song banter of Benjamin, the long dead singer from the Atlanta band Smoke: "Y'all be careful if you're driving, or if you can't be careful, be on the news."

***

Holiday cheer at the Dilly Dally. Conversation has taken the tone of a late-night freshman rap session with improbable questions, truth-or-dare? without the dare.

Everyone tries to achieve some semblance of verity without humiliation. Lots of sex and relationship questions and then as always, death pops up. How would you like to die? I say I would like to die like Robert Mitchum did: in his sleep and as Robert Mitchum.

14

Most people can't change. Someone might argue *won't* not *can't*, but *won't* allows more agency than I've witnessed. I only know from experience. Experience is anecdotal and therefore not proof. Experience is all most have, but it doesn't count according to reasonable people. I live beyond reason. It's quiet out here.

***

Men appear and vanish. Hookup ghost dance. I message with one who quizzes me about relationships. He's come out of one that he says was like an exchange of drunken prank calls.

 —Do you wish it could've been different?

 —I guess but I'd want to know how. I'd want a heads-up.

 He tells me he's liked talking with me, then spooks.

 Probably telling him I'd given up humanity for dead didn't help my chances. So what. It's only my future. That tired creation.

A man tells me his marriage troubles. The problem is he thinks he's in an opera but he's in a country song. The short version he can't bring himself to say: He and his husband are depressed, anxious people. They married so they could focus on one reason to be unhappy.

Another says, "I dreamed I worked on a bomb squad and ended up in one of those cut-the-yellow-wire scenarios, but I was color blind. What do you think it means sexually?"

***

On an app: Do I tell the guy saying he's an original thinker that I've heard that one before? I bail and check email. Spam subject line: "I've never had the strength to tell you" gives me the deathbed declaration scene I didn't even know I craved.

***

When we meet in person, we lower our voices an octave and talk loose jawed like food is falling out of our mouths. Butch queens.

***

Charlie says if you can find beauty in people's selfishness you can still love them, but if you can't it's best to sever all ties. Spare yourself the pain of their crushing unconcern. He mentions a romantic interest a few years back. "Something was off. I couldn't tell if he'd had face work, but anyone his age without a line on his face has either been cosmetically altered or never given a damn about anyone but themselves. Either way the psychological flaw is deep, and I have no need to fuck with it."

***

Overheard at the bar:
—Where you going?
—Don't know.
—Can I come with you?

***

Bathroom graffiti: Do you love me? Or am I a fantasy? Underneath: Open wide fag.

***

A man tells me he has a homemade glory hole. A sheet with a hole cut in it he hangs from his bedroom door. The buzzer sounds, he unlocks the apartment door, ducks behind his makeshift curtain. The trick closes the door, unzips, whips out his cock, and sticks it through the sheet. We both agree the allure of anonymous sex isn't the fantasy, the hunt, the capture. To lose yourself, shed your identity and thoughts, and be a series of motions and sensations is the glory.

***

My crossroads: where the bushy butch beard requires a dainty straw to drink anything.

The coffee shop is full of men with graying beards. We take off and put on our glasses to look at our phones and each other.

On the app, a young man: Do you have a hot dad voice?

Me: It's somewhere between congested Muppet and clinically depressed Paul Lynde.

I browse his photos. I love narcissists, but I don't expect them to notice. And I'm always slightly thrilled when I lose my crush on someone.

He probably doesn't know who Paul Lynde is. Those classic Hollywood Squares appearances are etched deep in my head.

Q: Paul, what is a good reason for pounding meat?

Paul Lynde: Loneliness!

Q. It is the most abused and neglected part of your body, what is it?

Paul Lynde: Mine may be abused, but it certainly isn't neglected.

I remember an old *Artforum* Top Ten list by Bruce Hainley where he refers to Paul Lynde's "snarling flamboyance." My life goals in two words.

***

When I see two men arguing in public, I assume that they are a couple and somewhere a French bulldog is blaming itself for the imminent divorce.

***

My young friend texts a photo of a man he likes.
—He's cute, right?

— If I were fifteen years younger, I'd be his funny friend with a raging, unrequited crush on him that I drunkenly cried about in the shower.

***

Mr. Nasty texts: The dirt under your nails in my mouth.
Me: When and where?
Silence.

***

The guy sends some pics, then a monologue: "I want someone who is loving and respectful to me and my friends and family and someone who is the romantic type as well as trustworthy and is private when it comes to showing affection. I don't think it's always important to show affection in public all the time, I think love more special when it's private anyway. I'm for someone who is caring not selfish or stubborn I don't like the cheating kind I'm happy to have threesomes, but it has to be talked out first, I don't like anyone who steals or lies. I also want a relationship with someone who doesn't base the relationship on money. A man who doesn't spend time with his family can never be a real man."

***

The guy sends a Blaise Pascal quote: "The strength of a man's virtue should not be measured by his special exertions, but by his habitual acts." Then a cock pic.

His bio says he's anti-war and ACAB, but he loves men in uniform. Also, workwear—he says the 65/35 cotton poly blend is boner city—and the standard denim fetish of a dickprint in tight Levi's 501 jeans. He acts as if these are niche fetishes rather than the entire waterfront.

***

My young friend complains about men. "These dudes all say they're tops, but then they can't deliver. Lie about their dick size, can't get it up, need Viagra, all the while talking like some kings of fuck."

"Everyone needs to calm the fuck down. The average dick is five to five and a half inches hard, the throat is five inches, and the prostate is two to four inches inside the rectum. It's not the Olympics or Mount Olympus. There are no heroes or gods. It's sex."

***

The essential, eternal question: Are you busy tonight?

***

Response to an ass pic: Love the intense pink corona around the beautiful slit of the actual asshole. A stunning male vulva to enjoy.
(Deletes app)

***

Charlie is deep in his sorting. He shows me an article about the bachelor tax in Argentina from around 1900. Men who could prove they had asked a woman to marry them and had been rejected were exempt from the tax. This gave rise to professional rejectors, women who for a fee would swear to the authorities that a man had proposed to them, and they had refused.

Charlie finds a 1993 newspaper clipping from the UK's Daily Mail entitled "Abortion Hope after Gay

Genes Findings" celebrating the discovery of the link between genetics and homosexuality. He adds them to a pile of articles—equally awful—about AIDS.

"Cocaine saved my life," he says. "I did so much coke I couldn't fuck. Coke dick was my AIDS miracle."

I don't mention I dreamed of Sam recently. He spun slowly on a pedestal, like a music box ballerina. Joyous and perfect, it wasn't sad, not until I woke up.

***

Last night, I stayed up late and watched a movie with smart dialogue and dumb violence. One punctuated the other until it became a game guessing whether the movie would end with words or blood. I fell asleep instead.

I dreamed about one of the actors. A minor character who carried his own light. That was how I had recognized him: his eyes. He had played young, fearful, teary men in police procedurals on TV. Since, he had bulked up and played hired killers and abusive boyfriends with dark childhoods shown in flashbacks.

Tonight, I will lie in bed and try to find the movie and stay awake long enough to watch the actor die or not die, kill or be killed, and shine.

***

Me to the falling snow and every man I've ever dated:
You are beautiful. Please don't stay.

15

After the long chaos comes this calm. It's inhuman.

The worst is over, I tell myself, and lift my head off the pillow. Once my feet are on the floor and I stand, it's too late. I have a sense my hands are solid. They are mine again. To someone who hasn't left their body, who has never viewed their body as an It, always as a Me, it's hard to explain. Not merely numb, although there has been plenty of that, too, but porous. The way the street noise has penetrated me, the people on the sidewalks have been aimed at me, or, worse, as if they are walking through me. The sense of myself as a place, not a person. Not the tourist and not the tourist attraction. Rather the place passed through on the way to the destination.

***

Talking on the phone with Greer I write down something she says offhand: The hopeless are hopeless. Meaning? Infestation becomes manifestation. What I thought was ubiquitous was ubiquitous because I thought about it everywhere I went.

I know there is a way out, something so simple it will stun me.

I think about a conversation with Avery that pissed me off but now offers comfort:

"You can't think about it too much," Avery said.

"How much is too much?"

"At all."

Pull back, back to the place I always have in these situations: the ceiling, the hall, the next building. From experience I know this will turn to scar tissue. Is that hope?

Let pain be pain. Don't transform. Don't rise above. Fry in its heat. And get up the next morning to spite it all.

***

Out of nowhere—by which I mean my phone—breaking radio silence, Dustin texts: I've been having vivid dreams lately. You've been in a lot of them. I wish things could go back to something. Something better. I miss you. I can't stop thinking about you. How are you?

I am drifting along downtown. My wandering interrupted by a long, angry truck horn. The barrage of the street overwhelms me. Sound throws up a wall. A man looks to the west while his two small boogery-eyed toy dogs sniff the urine-sodden pavement in search of the perfect spot to add their piss. Beauty and ugliness abound. A young guy in tight pants with a perfect fat ass turns with a jacked-up grin and mashed nose. A child is dragged along hiccupping sobs of no, no, no with snot dripping down its weak chin, blinking out tears from close-set eyes. Car horns and mindless chatter, and I look up at the bright blue, unreachable and perfect.

I want to tell Dustin I miss him and say how I am. Tell him how much time I've spent wondering what could have happened if he wasn't married and if we were at different places in our respective lives. Whatever different and respective mean, And places and lives too. These scenarios are romantic delusions not worth entertaining. Why have I? Loneliness, isolation, a character flaw, recidivism, addiction: multiple choice with no wrong answers.

The one-two punch: fear of love, love of fear.

I don't text back. My silence isn't a game. I truly don't know what to say. His text wants reassurance I miss him, and I do miss an idea of him and an idea of me. Missing isn't enough. I can't find the words and in the space where they should be is a perfect blank.

***

There is a novel with an anecdote I have used as my own over the years. On the last page of the book, the narrator recalls a story a friend told him about her peculiar near-sighted experiences. One night sitting at the far end of a bar she sees a man staring at her and she starts flirting suggestively with him to no avail. He continues staring in a noncommittal way. After another drink she decides to make the first move. She gets up and walks to his end of the bar but as she gets closer, she realizes the man is a stain on the wall.

I have told the story many times. Sometimes as having happened to a friend, other times to me. The telling depended on if I wanted to be merely funny or if I also wanted to disarm my audience. I told the anecdote to Dustin during a long night of stories and drinks. Now I wonder which of us was the stain.

***

When did I stop saying goodbyes? Probably five years ago when I realized it made no difference. Goodbyes slowed the exit.

I paint over the test stripes. Back to white. They still bleed through a bit, so I hang a sketch by Greer in a thrift store frame over them. I adorn it with a photo booth strip of Charlie and me taken at Pizza Shuttle.

My fantasy: I leave my keys at the bar, clean my apartment best as I can, though the landlord will find any excuse to keep my deposit, and have some money, not enough, but it will do.

I think of an interview with Leonard Cohen.

Interviewer: What happens next?

Leonard Cohen: I pick up my black bag and get on a plane.

***

Charlie's epic sell-off is complete. I joined him unloading books and clothes. Pennies on the dollar as my mother used to say. Both ridiculous—pennies and dollars.

"I thought you were rebuilding your library," Charlie said when I accompanied him to the used bookstore.

"I thought I was too, but I'd rather have the freedom," I said.

This time the freedom isn't snorted or injected. Simply less.

***

I peruse the work in Greer's studio. Vibrant streaks with figures turned away, bent over, lying with their backs to the viewer. Small photographs are grouped in pinned grids, some with similar poses. Two paintings are still under advisement, as Greer calls it. The leap from what I saw last fall until now shocks me. I've watched her pull off this trick before, but I know the cost and in the past, she had youth and a pissed-off drive. Now, the pace is different, the anger remains but as atmosphere more than directive.

She points to a grid. "Did you see yourself? It was when you fell asleep on my couch."

"I don't recognize myself, so I guess that means it is me."

***

I attend an ill-advised farewell party for a friend who has drifted away from me already. A formality. Someone complains about a mutual acquaintance freeloading at weekend houses, hopscotching sublets with strings attached. I want to say freeloading is a lot of work. Scraping and begging and beseeching and polite conversations and appeasing manners and making quick studies of people takes a toll. I say nothing because the talking man is supported by his boyfriend, and I know better than to wander in and cast a shadow on someone else's projection.

I slip out before the toast. On the corner, a coatless woman in a short skirt and a flimsy top argues with a man. She reels back drunk and angry, and her clothes compress. The skirt rides up and the top dips down. She yells, "All I want back is my dignity." I know how she feels.

On my walk, a stretch of three blocks is dark because the streetlights are out. The night sky becomes visible, but I don't recognize any constellations. I turn a corner into neon and fluorescence and the city is back again.

***

The car crawls, taking a route I'd rather not but I'm too underslept to bother complaining. I sit back and listen to parts of the terrible talk radio.

Last night, between bouts of regret about wasted time and the desperate things I've done to contain my loneliness, escape velocity was building, faint but steady.

A pulse. That pulse was what would save me. I knew it from long ago and it had always offered me refuge in its way: by forcing me to leave wherever I was, whatever I was calling home, by putting me back out into the world after what had usually grown stifling and small. The next thoughts had been about runaways as my sick little pattern. Another repetition. But look around, repetition and patterns are all I see. Our character flaws are in fact our characters.

I've done it before so many times, and sometimes I've felt most alive leaving, looking out the windows of cabs or trains or buses and thinking I belong here, and I will return and claim it again as mine. Other times I've left bereft or angry, certain I would never set foot in those places again.

This morning, I sip my coffee and watch the city, familiar and alien, as it passes. Something recedes, I'm not on my way to a plane or a bus. I have an all-day catering gig. I lean forward and say to the driver, "Could you put some music on?"

Acknowledgements

Parts of this book appeared in different forms in
The Anarchist Review of Books, *New World Writing*, *SCAB*,
Resurrection Mag, *Pale Blue Dot*, *Responses to Derek
Jarman's Blue*, and *Truant*. My thanks to all who
published them.

My gratitude to Richard Porter, Hedi El Kholti, Chris
Kraus, Robbie Dewhurst, Emily Hall, Eileen Myles,
Kate Zambreno, Robert Gluck, Jeff DeRoche, Erik
Moore, Matthew Kinlin, and John Lippens.

ISBN 978-1-7393649-6-0

Published in the U.K. by Pilot Press, 2024